UNINTENDED

Stories of Unforeseen Spankings

by

Lynn Carlyle

All Rights Reserved

2019 Lynn Carlyle

The characters, names and places in the stories are fictitious. Any resemblance to actual people or places are purely coincidental.

Contents

The Invitation 1
The Apology 24
The Great Manifest High School Athletic Caper and The Flippity Uppity Morning 37
The Suggestion 81

The Invitation

Eldon "Mack" McBride decided that he had to be experiencing one of the most serendipitous moments of chance he had known in his thirty years. He had just arrived days earlier in the first week of May in the very small town of Roustabout, Ohio. He had already begun setting up business in the property he had just purchased, and now he was going to actually have a chance to meet and talk to the young woman who was unquestionably the most fetching creature he had ever laid his eyes upon.

When he had arrived at the park in the small town where its annual festival was being held, he had done so primarily to get to know some people in the community. Roustabout was rather unfamiliar to him, as he had lived nearly all of his life in another small Ohio town twenty miles away. As soon as he arrived, he had encountered Sam Blasingame and his wife, Sam having been the real estate agent who had taken care of the seal of the recently acquired property.

Upon meeting for business, Mack and Sam had become friendly, so he joined them as they strolled around the festival. And it just so happened that when they approached an exhibitor table behind which the aforementioned young beauty was sitting at a table giving out information about her canoe livery business, Sam and his wife stopped to introduce Mack to someone who would be another rather young entrepreneur in the Roustabout community.

Paula Singleton stood when she saw the three of them approaching, and Mack was certain that it was not just his imagination that there seemed to be a little "something" in their lingering handshake and the exchange of glances upon the introduction. And just at that eventful moment, the Blasingames were called out to by a person at another vendor booth who wanted to speak to them. Paula

Downing asked the more than willing and interested Mack to sit down on an empty chair next to her.

Not only was she extremely pretty, she also was charming and soft-spoken, all of that part of an enticing package along with the quite long waves of black curls that fell down to the middle of her back. That was to say nothing of the exquisite figure, much of it revealed due to the quite short and low-cut pale blue sundress decorated with navy blue and white flowers.

Left alone for several minutes, they had already struck up quite a conversation. Mack found out that unlike him, she was a lifelong resident of the community, although that life encompassed only twenty-six years. Then it was to their mutual pleasure to realize that the property Mack had bought for his business was adjacent to the canoe livery business that Paula operated during the good weather in addition to her job as an elementary school teacher.

She went on to explain that her parents had operated the business that was situated upon the bank of the rather wide and often rapid Mickelson Creek that bordered both of their properties. When her parents had retired, also from teaching, they had moved to Arizona, giving her what had been her lifelong residence, the business and all. And throughout her entire life, a man by the name of Cyrus Benson had operated an auto body repair and paint shop on the adjacent property.

They discussed the fact that he was going to be living in the small house right next to the business, where Cyrus Benson and his wife had lived before retiring and moving away. He talked about how well-maintained the house was, and that he would have to do nothing to make it more than adequate for his own needs.

Although they had only known each other for a matter of minutes, their conversation was going along swimmingly and there was no doubt that there was an immediate, mutual attraction. And that was when Paula asked the question that changed the tone of everything. "So, when are you going to reopen the body shop?"

Max smiled and shook his head. "Oh, it's not going to be a body shop any longer. I'm converting it into the business I've wanted to open for a long time, ever since I was a teenager."

Paula smiled and leaned closer. "So, what kind of a business are you going to convert the place into?"

Max smiled, feeling much eagerness. "I'm going to open my own gun shop. I'm going to specialize in hunting rifles."

He sat perplexed as Paula leaned away, her jaw hanging wide open. "A gun shop?"

Suddenly the alluring face was filled with disgust. "We live in a country where people are killing each other left and right, and you're going to sell more guns to the public? And you want to sell more hunting rifles so that more gentle and helpless animals can be killed?"

Mack held up his hands defensively and laughed. "Hey, hey... I have to wonder if you ever eat a steak."

She clenched her teeth and nearly hissed her response: "It's not the same. Those animals are killed in controlled environments where they cannot be wounded to wander off and suffer until they die. I just think that hunting is so cruel. And it just sells more guns to people, the way things are these days...".

Suddenly she crossed her arms over her chest and looked away. "I don't want to talk to you anymore."

Feeling somewhat rattled, quite disappointed and also feeling an inexplicable twinge of amusement, Mack sighed deeply and theatrically, stood up shaking his head. He walked away and rejoined his previous companions, not telling them what had just taken place.

CHAPTER 2

It was not taking Mack very long to get what had been the body shop building retrofitted for his purposes. The building was constructed with concrete blocks, so turning it into a secure place to house weapons was not an elaborate task. He had to close off the front half of the building with the help of a construction crew he had hired to turn it into a presentable show room area. He was fairly proficient with wood work in his own right, so he was able to line the walls with wood paneling and construct the shelves upon which the long guns would rest to be on display.

He had also just received a delivery of some used but very well maintained glass display cases where the handguns would be offered for sale. And by the middle of June, he was already able to have his grand opening.

He felt a combination of emotions whenever he would peer across the property borders to see Paula working outside the canoe livery. She was often less 100 yards away from him, although there was no conversation between them. A couple of times he had shouted out a greeting to her, but she had always just turned her back and ignored him.

But it was difficult for him to ignore her. There was something about watching her work in arranging the canoes on the racks, the scenic stream in the background. Marliee Carson, another teacher and her close friend, worked as her assistant.

It was also made more difficult to ignore her due to the fact that most of the time when she was working outside in the good weather and her rush season was upon her, she would be sparingly clad in one of her bare midriff shirts with her business logo printed upon it, along with a rather revealing swimsuit bottom.

He certainly did not mind her chosen business uniform, although he realized that it was very practical for someone who was frequently wading into the edge of the stream to help launch customers in her canoes and bring them back into shore. She may have had an overly sassy and combative attitude about the things that she believed in, but Mack certainly had to give her credit for being a very hard-working person.

As he served his growing complement of customers in the comfort of a show room, she worked long hours outside, her tan deepening, the young woman showing that she was certainly not afraid of hard work. It was also not lost on him that she had a reputation in the community for providing wonderful customer service and being unfailingly devoted to the environment and nature in general.

He also could not help but enjoy the occasional moments when he looked out a window to see her in the distance playing with and exercising her collie. He kept such thoughts to himself, but he had to admit that he certainly would not mind having as much attention from her as that dog enjoyed.

On occasion the handsome dog would wander over onto his property, but he did not mind it at all. Mack hoped that someday it may manage to somehow bring them to have a second conversation. He simply did not know how true a manner in which that desire would one day be fulfilled.

CHAPTER 3

It was in mid-July, about fifteen minutes after he had closed his shop for the day after another profitable morning and afternoon, when he heard a knock on the door as he was adding up receipts for the day. He glanced up from the counter and noticed the front of the Sheriff cruiser through the opening of the window curtain. And when he opened the door, not only was there a pair of deputies, one male and one female, in the background an indignant looking Paula Downing stood with a look of smug satisfaction and her arms crossed across her chest in her usual and enticing outfit.

Mack's confusion was obvious as the female deputy spoke up: "Mr. McBride, your neighbor, Miss Downing here, has filed a complaint about your trash."

Mack looked back and forth between them and shook his head. "I don't understand, I put my trash in receptacles and I have a service that picks it up every week."

That was when Paula stepped forward and placed her hands on her hips and leaned forward in defiance. "And you're careless with it, and the breeze blows it into my backyard and around my buildings. I don't need that kind of a mess to clean up, and it's going to turn off my customers. You need to make sure the wind can't blow it around"

There was something about her attitude that seemed to go a little too far for Mack's tolerance level. "I bag up my trash, and sometimes I may have a raccoon or something get into it and tear it open. Sometimes I have to clean it up and put it in the new bag. But it's certainly not because I don't do my best to keep all tidy."

Her hands still on her hips, she walked closer to where Mack stood on the front porch of the business. "Well, see to it that you do. It's bad enough that you want to fill the countryside with more guns, I don't need to be picking up your trash."

The conversation at the festival seemed to intermingle with her over the top attitude at the moment, and something in it made Mack begin to boil inside. He was also aware that she had been making disparaging comments about the trash matter to others in the community. "Paula, there's no need for you to be that way."

She leaned closer. "You just don't like it because I have called you out for running an unethical business, and you just don't like that."

She stomped her foot and closed her fists, and that was when Mack spoke up again with a comment that even took him by surprise as it passed his lips: "I think that somebody ought to take one of those canoe paddles to your backside to teach you some manners."

Her face turned dark red, her cheeks filled with air and she turned to the deputies and motioned to Mack with a sweeping gesture. "Did you hear that? He just threatened to assault and batter me."

The male deputy was obviously struggling to keep from laughing, and he shook his head. "Miss Downing, I do believe that actually Mr. McBride simply made an expression of his opinion as to what should take place, rather than any statement of intent or any statement of such action being planned on his own right."

Then the female deputy chimed in. "And I would like to add, Miss Downing, you are certainly not making any case that what he just stated may not be true."

Paula spun back and forth in a fury, not knowing who to be the most angry with, her face beet red in her anger. "What is wrong with you people?"

Finally, she just pointed at Mack once again. "Just make sure your trash doesn't blow over on my property anymore."

Paula turned and walked away, her fists still clenched. And as the deputies left, Mack could not resist watching her wiggling departure, as he called out to her once again: "I still think that your canoes are not the only things that need paddled."

She stopped cold, turned around, clenched her fists and glared at him. Then she turned quickly and walked back to her property.

CHAPTER 4

They avoided each other for the next week, but Mack did take some time out of his busy week to pick an item from a display rack for his own use. It took him just a few minutes to attach the motion-activated trail camera to a post several feet away from his trash bin. He got busy again, and then three days later decided to end his day by downloading any images that may have been on the camera's memory storage chip. And when he did, it took him several minutes to stop laughing.

~~~

It was Saturday morning when Paula heard her phone chime to indicate that she had received a text message. She yawned on the sleepy morning that should have found her and her assistant hustling and bustling to launch canoes. But a heavy rainstorm accompanied by high winds had made canoeing impossible, and the same weather was predicted to last for three more days.

She sneered as she looked out the window to see that Mack's gun store parking lot was full, the lousy weather doing nothing to slow down his little corner of what she viewed as a national disgrace.

With a sigh, she plopped down on the sofa, curled her legs beneath her, and opened the message. To her shock, the message was from Mack, sent by way of her listed business number.

Actually, it was not a message in literal terms, for there were no words. But he had sent a photo… "Roscoe, no…" It was all she could mutter as she stared at the image of her collie tearing open the bag of trash behind Mack's house. Other images followed. The dog was able to clamp its teeth down on a trash bag and pull it out of the bin and scatter the contents across the back yard of Mack's place.

She found herself suddenly crying in regret and embarrassment such as she had never felt before. As she picked up her phone and simply held it motionless, her mind began to formulate the message she would send to him in return. And that was when her friend and assistant Marliee rang her doorbell, as they had decided to spend a quiet morning sharing some coffee and talking about everything and nothing.

~~~

Merilee leaned forward: "Oh my gosh, Paula, just how is it that you plan to apologize to him?" She smiled and arched her eyes. "If I were you, and I owed a hunk of a guy like him an apology, I would at least put on something sexy and take him a plate of cookies or something."

Paula laughed at her friend's comment, even though tears were forming in her eyes. "I know, he really is quite a picture of a man. And I have to admit, as much as I disapprove of how he makes a living, there's no question that when I met him at the festival and talked to him for a while, I was really strongly attracted to him right away."

"So how do you think you really going to handle this?"

Paula cleared her throat. "I think there's only one fitting way I can truly apologize to him, but I don't think I'm going to go into any more detail right now."

Marilee gasped at the comment: "You're actually going to…?"

Paula's face turned pink as her friend's question settled into her mind. "No, that's not what I mean. Let's just let it go with saying that there's sort of a little inside joke between he and I that I intend to turn into a more serious matter. So, this afternoon, I'm going to do a couple of things to get ready and send him a message."

~~

Late on that Saturday afternoon, Paula read back over the text before she hit send: **Mack, I know that neither of our businesses will be open tomorrow afternoon, and I decided to take the chance that perhaps you would be willing to come here around 3:00.**

I feel the need to apologize to you in a quite fitting and appropriate manner, and then after we have spent the afternoon addressing my behavior, we can share an elegant dinner consisting of a frozen pizza I have been saving for a special occasion, a bag of chips and some rather inexpensive but quite enjoyable wine. Hope that you can accept this invitation and the very special apology that I plan to offer.

She sent the message on its way, and less than ten minutes later her phone chimed with the response from Mack: **No man in his right mind would turn down an invitation to spend time with a beautiful young woman such as yourself, a woman that I believe is really rather kindhearted and very interesting to talk to. I am looking forward to it, but I am wondering if you're going to give me a hint about this mysterious apology.**

Paula took a deep breath, leaned over to the other end of the sofa where an object rested that she had gone to the basement to find earlier that morning, and took a picture with her phone. She typed a quick message before she lost her nerve and set it to Mack.

It took a little while for Mack to be able to see that message, as he was waiting on some customers who had come into his store. An hour after the message had been sent to him, he was finally alone as he chuckled at the photo she had sent and read her caption: **Mack, it would not actually be practical, nor cost-effective, for me to actually cut the handle off one of my precious oars. But I did remember seeing something in a box of old toys in the basement the other day. I removed the long rubber band and rubber ball to prepare it for your very necessary and well-deserved use.**

When you come here tomorrow, just come on in the house. I will be standing in front of the sofa waiting for you, the sofa upon which you can make use of this little antique item all afternoon to fully accomplish my apology to you.

He felt more than a little uncomfortable that he was experiencing undeniable arousal as he read the message. He stared at the photograph of the decades old small paddle that Paula had likely enjoyed for many hours in her childhood, trying to keep the little rubber ball bouncing back and forth.

His response was simple: *Now I can't wait. See you at your sofa at 3:00.*

Less than two hundred yards away, Paula was reading his response and trembling in a combination of fear and an excitement that made her feel uncomfortable. For some reason, it bothered her that going to the basement to retrieve the little paddle had made her feel more than a little turned on.

And in the process of sending those messages to Mack, she was having a more intense session of those feelings. And reading his acceptance of the invitation and his obvious eagerness for the moment to arrive, made her body quiver inside. And beyond all reason and common sense, she was in unquestionable, eager anticipation herself. She doubted that she would be able to go to sleep that night.

~~~

Paula did manage to sleep for about half of the night, and she had no way of knowing that it was pretty much the same case for Mack. When she finally decided it was time to get out of bed and begin what was certain to be a momentous day through which she would question her own sanity nonstop, one more idea came to mind.

She had a light breakfast, then began one more task to be ready for Mack's arrival later that day. She would have been quite amused if she could have seen the smile on her face as she worked on her special little project that only took a minute.

~~~

Mack spent most of that morning and then the early afternoon trying to convince himself that the matter of the paddle had just been a teasing joke, a fitting follow-up to the comments he had made to her when she had brought the authorities to his door about the trash. He would simply have to give her credit for being clever, and he reasoned that it would be illogical to expect that they were going to be doing anything other than sitting and talking before having dinner together.

He kept himself busy straightening his gun store until it was almost time to go to her house. There was a heavy rain falling once again, so he got into his pickup truck and made the brief journey to her house that was located a couple of hundred feet away from the canoe livery.

He stepped up onto the front porch, finding himself surprisingly nervous as he recalled what she had said about his arrival. He opened the door and stepped inside, and there she was. Just as she said she would be, she was standing in front of the sofa in the living room where all the blinds and curtains had been drawn closed.

She was holding that small paddle in front of her, and as he stepped closer, he could see that she was unsuccessfully attempting to fight back tears. But then a meek smile appeared on her face as she allowed her hands to fall to her side so that he could read her shirt.

It was not just any shirt: it was one of her little logo shirts cut short to reveal her midriff, quite a fetching complement to the bathing suit bottom she was wearing, one obviously more brief than those she usually wore outside when tending to her work.

They both began to smile as he read the large letters on her shirt. It was a white shirt with large black lettering proclaiming: "Want To

Paddle With Paula?". The phone number and website of the business was printed in smaller letters and numbers below.

What was most notable was how her business slogan had been altered. The word "With" had been crossed out with a black marker, the remaining words asking simply: "Want To Paddle Paula?".

She handed him the paddle, then he slid the handle of it inside a pocket on his khaki slacks. He placed his hands on her shoulders, feeling somewhat rattled to see tears rolling down her cheeks: "You're serious about getting this paddling, aren't you?"

She exhaled a deep breath and nodded her head slowly, managing to smile in spite of her emotions: "Hey, I don't dress like this for just any occasion."

She began to cry even harder. "Mack… I am just so sorry. You have a right to have a gun shop, and I have now realized I wasn't looking past that to see the kind of guy you really are.

"And I feel horrible about talking to other people around here about you the way that I did. And that silly dog of mine… Roscoe is just such a bad, bad boy."

She surprised him by reaching her hands around his waist and hugging him. "And I seem to have been such a bad, bad, bad girl. So I think that you know what needs to happen to a bad, bad, bad like I've been."

He leaned his head down and touched his nose to her, causing her to giggle. "Just asking one more time, you mean for this to be for real?"

She leaned her head back and wiped another tear from her cheek: "Yes, and we have a lot of time before dinner for you to make sure that when this is over, I will feel that I have been soundly and adequately chastised."

He took a deep breath and reached back for the paddle, and she stepped back and made a grand sweeping gesture toward the sofa: "And now, my good man…before I lose my nerve and chicken out…".

Feeling nervous in his own right, Mack sat down in the middle of the sofa. He felt that as Paula knelt next to him and then slithered across his knees to settle into place to be paddled, he thought that he had never seen anything quite so enticing and sensuous, and that was not making any sense to him at all. After all, he was about to commence with paddling her, not something that was intended to have sexual overtones.

At the same time, Paula waited nervously to feel the first stinging smack the small paddle had to offer. She was still confused as to why deciding that it was only fair and just that she get her tail extensively warmed had caused her to feel so darned turned on since the morning. Now the anticipation and knowing that her paddling was about to begin at any moment only made those sensations begin to stir more deeply inside of her.

As she felt Mack softly patting the paddle against the center of her bottom, she clenched her teeth and squeezed her eyes closed. It was purposeful that she had selected a white bikini bottom to wear that was more than a thong, but still skimpy enough to ensure that there would be nothing between her tender backside and the paddle. And then, for the first time, she felt the effects of her accumulative decisions over the past twenty-four hours.

The sharp SMACK was unsettling as the warm sting bloomed across the center of her bottom. And then, spaced several seconds apart… SMACK… SMACK… SMACK… SMACK… SMACK!

He leaned close and spoke softly. "Those must have really stung. You seemed to start squirming. And we're just getting started." SMACK… SMACK… SMACK… SMACK… SMACK!

Now she was beginning to suck in her breath each time the paddle landed. She was realizing in no uncertain terms that she had underestimated the extent to which the lightweight, teardrop shaped instrument of thin plywood could scorch its tender target upon impact.

Her eyes popped wide open when she felt the paddle rest upon her lower back and his right hand began to softly caress her paddled bottom cheeks. Even though the initial smacks of the small paddle had stung significantly, she could not believe just how delightful and sensuous the caressing of his hand was feeling at that moment.

She looked back at him and smiled. "So I guess it is going to take all afternoon for you to give me this paddling, especially if you keep that type of thing up."

He laughed and leaned toward her as the caressing continued: "Well, I believe you said that this may take most of the afternoon to accomplish. I just thought that it may help you cope with your paddling. Of course, I wouldn't have to do this gentle stroking...".

She looked back and shook her head rapidly. "Oh, no, I don't want you to stop doing this. You can pause the paddling and do this whenever you want."

She found herself stunned at her words. This was turning out to be an entirely different type of experience than she had in mind when the idea of taking a paddling from Mack first surfaced in her consciousness. Was she now coming on to him while he was paddling her?

Now it was the flat surface of the paddle caressing her bottom. She found it exciting and forbidden that his actions were making her hunger for the painful smacks to resume. How could she find something painful to be arousing?

She was lost in her thoughts, so it took her by surprise when the paddling resumed, but with significantly increased force... CRACK!

She let out a yelp, feeling disappointed in herself for expressing discomfort in receiving something she had insisted upon. CRACK... CRACK... CRACK.

She found it strangely fascinating that they were suddenly partners in bringing about significantly increased pain to her flesh, yet she was feeling turned on and challenged by it, even as it continued... CRACK... CRACK... CRACK... CRACK... CRACK... CRACK... CRACK...CRACK. He paused for a moment and tapped her several times before... WHAM!

She had to strain to muffle her cry, as well as when the next one landed with just as much force... WHAM... WHAM... WHAM... WHAM... WHAM.

He saw that she was wiping her eyes, so he reached into his pocket and leaned toward her and handed her his handkerchief. Now his left hand was stroking her back, while the paddle was being shuffled slowly back and forth across the now red bottom cheeks that were simply sizzling.

"I took it that you meant that I should give you the tanning you had coming."

She sniffled and looked back at him and nodded her head. "And that's exactly what I expect you to do."

He tapped her several more times. "Funny thing, I know that you have a lot more coming, and I plan to give it to you, but right now I just have this totally irrational desire to just rub my hand over your hot, red bottom for a while."

She murmured and purred like a kitten when he placed the paddle on the sofa and began to stroke his right hand back and forth in a circular manner across her now well paddled bottom. And at the same time, his left hand was stroking her back, and he had even pushed her short little top up nearly to her shoulders so that his hand could be in contact with more of her flesh.

Before she could catch herself, she gave her bottom a couple of wiggles. "Uhhmm… I guess I'm really liking that stroking. I guess I seemed kind of forward."

His stroking suddenly extended down to the tops of her thighs, his gentle touches expanding in territory. "Actually, it seems like what we are doing, and the way in which it is being done, is in and of itself quite intimate." He surprised her with a sharp smack of his hand, causing her to jump, although she laughed as well.

He caressed for a few seconds more, then surprised her yet again with an even harder smack of his hand. Now when the stroking resumed, he thought that he could feel her softly pressing her bottom up slightly as if she wished to increase the friction of his flesh upon hers.

He began to rub his hands across the hot, sore cheeks more roughly for a minute before raising his hand up and returning it with a loud… CRACK… CRACK… CRACK… CRACK… CRACK… CRACK!

Now he was stroking her again, and in the nearly silent room he could hear her nearly whisper… "Oh… my… gosh… Oh, wow… Wow… Wow… Wow!"

He began to stroke once more, but then suddenly they began to talk about everything that had happened to bring them to that point. Paula recounted how she had become so illogically upset in finding out that Mack was going to be opening a gun shop. She talked about how she had felt so immediately attracted to him until the moment he had told her that.

She looked back at him, sighed a deep breath, then lowered her face onto her forearms and settled in and awaited as Mack picked up the paddle once again… SMACK… SMACK… SMACK… SMACK… SMACK…… SMACK.

Once she had collected her wits about her once more, she began to talk about how she had so immediately assumed that he was being careless with the trash, and that was when Mack began to truly understand the manner in which she needed to get past the behavior she now also regretted and felt so embarrassed by.

She finished that segment of her story, a conversation that had gone on for nearly fifteen minutes, before she once again looked back at him wistfully. She looked forward and lowered her chin once more and settled in as Mack picked up the paddle and tapped her several times.

The warning taps having been applied, Mack seemed quite stunned at how her body seemed so relaxed as yet another round of painful whacks was about to begin.. She did not tense up as she awaited the first... CRACK, nor did her body betray any distress as it continued... CRACK... CRACK... CRACK... CRACK.

He saw her pressing the handkerchief to her eyes, but nonetheless she did not flinch or make many audible sounds as it continued... CRACK... CRACK... CRACK... CRACK... CRACK... CRACK... CRACK. He gave her yet another fifteen solid swats before he set the paddle aside and began to caress away some of the burn from the now crimson bottom.

The next conversation was lengthy, going on for nearly forty-five minutes without a single smack being applied to her bottom, although it was caressed continuously to their mutual enjoyment. She spoke endlessly about how she had so recklessly and thoughtlessly aired her grievances about Mack to others in the community.

She spoke as to how everyone took her word, everyone sided with her point of view because she was a well-known, local person. She talked about how she had been proud of herself up to this point, having established a reputation as an accomplished teacher at the local school, and the fact that her canoe livery brought more tourists and revenue into the community.

She cried again as she talked about how she was going to see to it that people found out how wrong she had been about Mack, and how she had misused their trust in her and her good reputation to lodge petty grievances over things he was innocent of. But also thrown into the conversation was some talk about how they hoped to begin to see each other, both of them acknowledging that it was not at all out of the question that they could form a very interesting relationship.

Both of their hearts were buoyed by that part of the discussion, but by the time that Paula had spent nearly ninety minutes across Mack's knees being alternately paddled, caressed, forgiven, cheered up and paddled some more, her thoughts and words kept returning to what weighed most heavily upon her mind: she had been grossly unfair to Mack and cast him in a negative light to so many others.

Yielding to the inevitable conclusion as he continued to caress her barely cooled off butt, Mack sighed deeply and dramatically, then spoke to her in a stern voice. "Then it seems to me, Paula, that we need to finish up by my giving you a long, hard paddling."

He watched carefully as he picked up the paddle from the sofa, and he saw an almost imperceptible nod of her head as she settled back in, this time laying her cheek upon her interlaced fingers to await something that they both knew needed to be memorable.

The paddle landed across her right cheek with such robust force behind the impact that she gasped out loud. But every one that followed was to be just as fiery in its sting and frightening in the sound that it made. It did not take very many before she was once again dabbing at tears, but this time the paddling was so hard, so intense, not much time being given between whacks for her to cope.

She burst into sobs, but still she struggled to stay in place and fight the urge to try to bring this paddling to an end before Mack decided she had had enough. Two minutes into the paddling, Mack was making it clear that she was still far from having been paddled long and hard enough. But both of them knew that he was doing so for the purpose of bringing her resolution with herself, as well as with Mack.

She was not about to ask him to back away from the intensity of the long and hard whacking she was getting. Nor was he about to take any chances of her going to bed that night feeling that he had fallen short in seeing to it that she felt that true and adequate justice had been applied to her backside.

The paddle continued to slam down across her enticingly plump bottom cheeks, the shade of crimson now a darker hue. After one especially memorable... WHACK... Mack allowed his hand to linger a moment, the fingers wrapped around the handle on the paddle detecting the warmth rising from her bottom.

The paddle had landed extra hard several dozen times during this final paddling, and yet there had been only perhaps three times that afternoon when Paula had audibly reacted to the sting of a hard smack. And suddenly it was over, as she laid there crying and wiping the tears from her face, but both of his hands were again caressing her soft skin, neither of them in a hurry for her to move at all.

She lay there across his knees for another half hour. About ten minutes into that they began to talk about what had taken place on that remarkable day, and then some more about what could be awaiting them in the coming days and weeks. And each of them spoke in a manner that it was clear they assumed that there was much more to come in terms of a relationship.

Finally Mack helped Paula up to kneel next to him again, and they talked some more about their most unusual day, a day that still was to transition into dinner and the evening to come. Suddenly they both went silent, and somehow they found themselves in an embrace, engaged in a long kiss that found their tongues intertwining with each other's.

When the kiss ended, they gazed at each other for a few seconds, their faces just inches away. Paul sighed and arched her eyes and shook her head. "Seems that I have indeed been a bad, bad, bad girl." Then she smiled as Mack tapped her on the nose.

"So what else do you have to say for yourself, young lady?"

Somehow, under the circumstances, she managed a smile like a pixie as she responded: "Ouch!"

Slowly they got up from the sofa and they began to walk toward the kitchen. Even after the remarkable circumstances of the day, they decided it was time to go ahead and put the frozen pizza in the oven, open the bag of potato chips and pour some wine. But when she pulled the pizza from the freezer on top of the refrigerator, she placed it on the counter and they were once again wrapped in another tight embrace, sharing another deep kiss.

Mack ran his fingers through her black waves and curls and shook his head. "Do you think we are ever going to do anything like that again?"

She looked at him, her mind obviously weighing a serious question. "I don't know. But I do know myself, so I don't think there's much question that the time will come when I at least I deserve a good paddling again."

Now both of them were laughing. "I just have this funny feeling, Mack... I have this feeling that I may look back upon this afternoon and for some reason I can't explain, find myself yearning to experience at least some of it again."

She put her arms around his neck and gazed up at him. "So tell me, Mack...in the case that I may find myself in need of a good paddling again someday, can I count on you to deliver?"

Her answer was immediate, as his hand reached around behind her and collided with her bottom with a loud... SMACK!

Her eyes wide open, she reached back and rubbed her bottom while managing a mischievous grin. "I guess I can live with that response."

      THE END

The Apology

As Tom Eldridge sat at his desk in the office he shared with his father in the back of the paint store, he heard the familiar footsteps of his approaching partner in the business. "Hey, Dad."

Max Eldridge at fifty-five looked very much like his son. Tom was thirty and had opened the store five years before with the help of a large business loan. And right away he and his wife Elaine had encouraged Max and Tom's mother Marcia to join them in the enterprise.

The timing had been crucial: Max had just been let go as a production supervisor at an automotive component plant. Even though he had received a generous severance package, he still had several years to go before for retirement, and Tom convinced everyone to make the best of the situation and come together in the new enterprise.

Max stepped up and put his hand on Tom's shoulder: "The shipment of new wood stain is going to be delayed a day. Just wanted you to know that."

Tom turned around with a look of concern. "Dad, you seem kind of down. Are you feeling okay. I can hear in your voice even that something isn't right."

Max smiled and patted his son on the shoulder. "We can talk about it later, okay? I think the supply truck is about to arrive, so your mother and I are going to be busy putting the new brushes and rollers on the shelves and in the storeroom. We can talk later."

Throughout the rest of the day, Tom was bothered by his father's demeanor. And as soon as Elaine had walked to the front door and locked it and turned on the sign that told everyone in a neon green that the store was "Closed", Tom looked around to find Max. But before he had gotten up from his desk, Elaine leaned in the door.

Her wide smile and the long wavy brunette hair was all he needed to lift his spirits as she called out to him: "I'm going to head on to the house. I know you're going to be here for a while, so I'll get something out of the freezer and into the microwave. Love you."

Tom smiled and called back to her. "Love you too!" He leaned back in his chair a little bit, trying in vain to get a glimpse of the back of her as she walked away. They had been married for eight years, but he could not get enough of watching that wonderful sway of her bottom in blue jeans. He shook his head and laughed at himself, then got up and went to look for his father.

~~~

The two men ended up meeting in the storage room where the coffee maker was stationed. They both felt a bit of relief in that Saturday afternoon had finally arrived, and a couple of part-time assistants would be taking care of the store on Sunday, although Tom would always have his cell phone at the ready in case any problems arose. But he and Elaine were looking forward to a quiet evening together, hopefully expending some pleasurable effort in starting a family, Tom hoping that that desirable task would spill over into the next morning as well.

Tom and Max each poured a cup of coffee, and Tom nodded with his head toward the door that led to the office. "Okay Dad… I think we should go into the office and enjoy some coffee and I want you to tell me what's bothering you."

Tom noticed that his father turned somewhat pale and nodded in agreement, but his reluctance to discuss what was on his mind was apparent. They entered the office and both of them grabbed a desk chair and pulled them close to each other and began to sip at the coffee. Sensing that his father was reluctant to open up about what was troubling him, Tom decided to break the ice. "Okay, Dad... I need to know what's going on with you."

Max leaned forward with his coffee in his hands and sighed deeply. "Tom, I guess I was always a little concerned about something like this... I guess people have said that a family going into business together held the potential for some extra... I guess I should say, issues.

"I am so reluctant to make a comment to another man about his wife, even my own son...".

Tom leaned forward and placed his hand on his father's knee. "Dad, it's okay. So what is it that you have to say to me about Elaine?"

Max closed his eyes and leaned back in the chair and shook his head. "Tom, I hate to bring this up but... I have to. You see, Marcia came to me after work yesterday and she was crying."

Tom leaned closer: "Why was Mom crying? Something to do with Elaine?" Tom felt a chill as he saw his father nod his head slowly and reluctantly. He dearly loved Elaine, and could not see himself with any other woman.

She was sweet and loving and bright and witty and would not hurt another person in the world...with the exception that she seemed to lose her filter and manners around her mother-in-law, Marcia. And it was something that Tom and Elaine had discussed several times over the years.

Max continued: "I know we've talked about some little incidents before... I just was bothered by how upset your mother was last evening. I guess that she and Elaine were rearranging some of the color samples on the display, and your mother got a row of them out of order in the earth tones. And she told me that Elaine made a comment to her that that type of thing happened too many times and that someone who is colorblind probably shouldn't be working in the paint store."

Tom sat in stunned silence for a moment. "Dad, I'm so sorry. I have never been able to fully understand what Elaine's problem is with Mom. As much as I love Elaine, I know very well that Mom has never done anything to justify some of the comments Elaine has made to her. And for this one especially, there is no justification at all.

"I've been upset with some of the other things she has said to Mom. And I can't understand why she can't give Mom the benefit of the doubt. And we all know that Mom is not colorblind. I have to admit that my own wife was so unjustifiably mean-spirited… I have to say, once again.

"Dad… I promise I'm going to have a very serious talk with Elaine tonight."

Max groaned and shook his head. "In the past, Marcia really has never wanted me to make an issue of any of Elaine's remarks or putdowns. But none of them before ever left her in tears. I know this is really getting to her, because when I told her I intended to talk to you about it, she agreed to that, where every other time she has pleaded with me to just try to keep things smooth and quiet."

Tom stood up and Max did as well, and Tom stepped over to his father and gave him a hug. "Dad, please tell Mom I'm so sorry about this. I will do everything I can within reason. Most importantly, I want you and Mom to know that I have never had a second thought about the moment I asked the two of you to be involved in this business with us. I could not have better business partners than the people who raised me and served as my role models."

~~~

The drive home from the store to the house that Tom and Elaine lived in was only two miles, but the journey on this day seemed to take forever. It was foremost in his mind what he and Elaine had planned for the evening after a nice dinner out.

But no matter how much she argued or tried to insist that the problem was being blown out of proportion, this time she was going to have to deal with the reality of what affect she was having upon her in-laws and the business, as well has her husband's peace of mind. And Tom could not dispel the thought that had been bouncing around in his mind for some time about what may bring about a needed change in her behavior.

As he pulled his car to the garage and turned off the engine, he sat in the dimly lit garage for a moment to think. He knew how this usually had played out before: Tom had walked into the house to talk to Elaine about her latest mistreatment of Marcia, only to have her get her back up in protest and issue some kind of justification for what she had said or done.

But this time, Tom was not about to accept any such excuses, even if their evening got ruined and the start of their family got postponed. There may very well be no nice dinner at a nice restaurant this evening.

Just as he was about to open the door, his phone chimed with a special tone that told him he was receiving a text from his father: ***Tom, very happy that Elaine called Marcia to apologize. Seems that they talked for quite a while, and I understand it was good.***

Tom sat in confusion for a moment. This was not the typical pattern followed when Elaine had in the past breached good decorum with the older woman.

He got out of the car, for some reason feeling the need to do so quietly. He took the three steps from the garage up into the kitchen, and opened the door slowly, entered and closed it in similar silence. He walked slowly through the kitchen and into the living room, and gazed upon Elaine standing in front of the large living room window and looking out. She appeared to have her arms crossed in front of her.

She was wearing a red dress with a black floral pattern, one he had not seen before. It was exceptionally short compared to the rest of her wardrobe, and he knew that it had been picked out especially for a night of marital romance. Even under the circumstances, he was bewitched by the vision of her that way, the long brown wavy hair flowing down below her shoulders. He took a purposely louder step into the room and she turned around.

Her face was somewhat pale, although her eyes were rimmed in red as she rushed toward him with her arms out. They embraced tightly and she laid her head against his shoulder. "Tom… I really screwed up."

She grasped his hand and led him to the sofa and they sat down. She took a deep breath and began to talk, her eyes barely open. "You know what happened …I mean, do you know what I said to Marcia and how I talked to her?"

Even though Tom felt a strange sense of relief in seeing her upset at her own actions, he felt that this was the best opportunity ever to press home the points that had to be made. "You mean yesterday, or all the times before?"

Her expression was one of contrition as she bit down on her lower lip and nodded her head. "Okay, I had that coming. But for right now, I'm referring to what I did yesterday.

She kicked her shoes off and leaned back and placed her feet on the coffee table. She began to speak, then hesitated.

She suddenly sprung from the couch and began to pace the floor, beginning to cry. "All day long this has been eating away at me. I tried to pretend around Marcia all day today that nothing had happened. And of course, Marcia didn't bring anything up, like she never does when I treat her like crap." Tom was stunned to hear her describe her own behavior in that way, but he sat there in silence as she continued to pace the floor and cry.

"This morning when I woke up it was like all of a sudden I realized how needless it was for me to say what I did...I mean, not just yesterday but all those times before. And I had accused her of getting the color samples in the wrong order, and I was my usual rude self. Something about it today just struck me as to how much Marcia really means to all of us.

"I guess I was just thinking ahead to the day when we have a family. For some reason I was able to put myself in her place, thinking about if we had a son and his wife started acting like a bitch to me.. I would feel unwelcome and empty." She began to cry harder and pressed her fingers to her temples. "And that's what I've been doing to her.

"I don't know what it was for sure, Tom. I think I just saw this hurt look on her face when we left the store yesterday. And when I woke up this morning, I saw it again and I realized what it meant and why it was so unfair, and I felt ashamed of myself."

She turned to face him and began to cry harder. "And guess what, Tom? I realized today I was the one who had made the mistake on the color samples. So, I called Marcia and apologized.

"But I still feel so rotten about myself. There's no one who can help me get past that other than you, Tom. But I don't know what to ask you to do. I don't know what you can say to me."

She began to wipe her eyes, and Tom got up from the sofa and walked toward her and put his hands on her waist. "I must say, I've been wanting to hear you say something like that for a very long time."

Suddenly Tom could not tell if she was laughing or crying and she gestured down toward the new dress she was wearing. "We were going to have this nice evening together, hopefully having a nice dinner and some hot sex to try to get a family started." She started crying even harder as she reached down to the hem of her dress and pulled it out to both sides. "I was hoping this dress would even help set the mood."

Tom sighed heavily and took her hand in his and they walked back to the sofa and sat down. "Elaine, honey… I think it's time you heard me say some things that I mean from the heart, but I need to be very blunt with you."

She bit down on her lip again and nodded her head. "I think that would be best, yes. I want you just say to me everything that needs to be said."

He put his knuckle under her chin and raised her head to face him and he smiled, then leaned forward and placed a kiss on her lips. "First of all, you could be wearing a feed bag and I would want to fool around with you. And I've been waiting for this too, for the effects of the pill to wear off and we felt that we could really go at it and start a family." He enjoyed seeing her blush at his reference.

"At the same time, although I am very pleased to hear you say the things you have said right now about your realization about your behavior, we need to make sure these things don't happen again. I understand from what you just said, that's how you feel too."

She blew out a deep breath and nodded her head in agreement. "That's right. I don't want it to happen again, but I'm also dealing with feeling so badly about what already has happened, words that I can't take back."

Tom sat for a moment with his elbow resting on his knee and his chin resting upon his fist as he pondered his next words. She looked at him with curiosity, uncertain as to what to make of his expression. Finally, he spoke, although she could sense his reluctance to say what exactly he had on his mind.

He turned slightly to face her and placed his hand on her knee. "Elaine, I've been thinking about this for a while… I think I need to give you a very hard and lengthy spanking."

He was surprised that she did not in any way express any look of shock or objection. To his amazement, she closed her eyes, bit down on her lip and nodded as if she was agreeing with him as he continued. "And we would do this, knowing that if it ever occurred again, I would do the same thing in response."

She cleared her throat and began to rub her hands together atop her knees. "Tom… I can't say that I've ever envisioned myself getting a spanking it age thirty. And at the same time, in the past I never envisioned myself treating a woman like your mother the way I've treated her. Sometimes I wonder if maybe I feel some resentment because I had always hoped we would make it on our own in business without any help from your parents."

Tom reached over and put his hand on her shoulder. "Elaine… I only suggested we invite them to be partners because I knew they were so trustworthy. It's not like they helped us finance the business. They haven't put any more cash into the operations than we have. We could have asked anyone else to partner with us."

He leaned back for a moment. "You've never spoken like that to my father."

She closed her eyes and shook her head back and forth. "No, I guess I wouldn't have dared to." She looked up and smiled meekly and apologetically. "I guess I just felt that your mother was a softer person I could vent my frustrations upon. And I guess that takes us back to the fact that I've treated her badly, and I feel rotten about it."

Her face turned pink and she closed her eyes and blew out a long deep breath. "I guess that if a thirty-year-old woman ever deserved a good spanking, I'm the one. And Tom, I'm not going to argue, I'm not going to whine or ask you to not do it. I've had this coming for a long time." She began to laugh softly. "It may take a couple of days, but I'm probably going to feel better about myself after this happens."

She looked at him and grimaced. "I only have one request… I would like for us to do this right away… I would like to get this done and over with right now." She squeezed her eyes shut and grimaced once again. "Please?"

Tom felt a twinge of guilt in that he almost laughed at the face she made, and also that he was looking forward to doing this a little too much. "I agree. Right now." He looked at her to see her simply nodding in agreement.

He placed his hand on her knee and gave it a squeeze. "I'm going to close the curtains, and I would like for you to go and get that wooden hairbrush on your dresser that has been screaming at me for a while now to make good use of it." To his surprise, she almost laughed, but she simply winced and shook her head, got up from the couch and walked toward the bedroom.

It seemed to Tom that she had been gone from the now dimly lit room for only seconds before she appeared back in front of the sofa with the hairbrush in her hand. He scooted over into the center of the sofa and patted the cushion to his right, and her shoulders appeared to slump as she crawled onto the sofa and knelt next to him.

Without his telling her to, she laid down across his knees, then he noticed she had a handful of tissues. Obviously she was correctly anticipating the seriousness of what she was about to receive from her anticipation that the hairbrush was going to be used with great emphasis. She felt his hand caressing her bottom through the back of the dress and he whispered to her: "I love you."

She turned her head and looked back at him and managed to smile, although tears were forming in her eyes: "I love you too. And I'm ready, honey."

As she expected, Tom whisked her dress up to her waist, but to her surprise he began to tap the hairbrush against her bottom without first lowering her panties. Then she no longer felt the brush, and she held her breath until for the first time the brush collided with her bottom with a sharp... CRACK.

A cry of... "Ouch" followed the first smack, but only a couple of seconds later both sounds were repeated identically. Over and over the same sounds filled the room... CRACK... "Yikes"... CRACK... "Ouch"... "CRACK... "Yikes"... CRACK..."Ooowwoo!.

Tom found it somewhat remarkable that her expression of pain each time the hairbrush made impact was rather controlled, except that the decibel level of her verbal response was increasing each time. Even when the hairbrush had landed for a full two dozen times, her response was in the same measured tone.

That all changed when he paused to take a moment to perform the task she had expected to take place at the beginning of her paddling. That was when she felt him reach for the waistband of her panties and yank them down rather unceremoniously to her knees.

From that moment on, her verbal responses were varied, urgent, desperate and loud, for not only was she now absent one very thin layer of nylon between the hairbrush and her bottom, that hairbrush was now colliding with her tender flesh with much more force and speed. Now she was squealing and crying out each time the hairbrush made its fiery, stinging landing upon the bottom that was already quite red and sore.

Now she was finding that her decision to make her way to the sofa with a handful of tissues had been most wise. She dabbed at her face constantly, blowing her nose when she had a chance to catch a breath.

And when the hairbrush stopped its fiery assault after it had cracked with its sizzling impact upon her bare bottom for the fortieth time, the sobbing Elaine simply laid across her husband's knees to recover. All the while, he stroked her back with his left hand and tried to calm her with soothing caressing of the backs of her thighs.

Finally, he could tell that she was ready to get up, so he gently helped her up to kneel on the sofa. Immediately she collapsed against his chest, sobbing and apologizing once again.

It took her a while to finally calm down as he held her tightly against his chest, stroking her and running his hands through her long hair. Finally, she spoke in a whisper through her labored breathing. "No...hard...chairs...order... pizza...delivered."

After a few more minutes, she was calm, and she leaned away and turned her back to him and spoke softly while also sliding her panties the rest of the way off: "Zipper, please." Highly amused and fully aroused, Tom eagerly but carefully lowered the zipper of the sexy new dress and helped her pull it off over her shoulders to form a colorful puddle at her waist.

She finally smiled and reached behind with both hands and deftly unhooked her bra which dropped on top of the dress. She stood up and everything fell to the floor. Standing naked, her bottom aglow, she took Tom by the hand, and when he stood, she led him into the bedroom.

~~~

Her head on his chest, she smiled and caressed his abdomen. "I don't know if the conception odds were altered by me being on top, but there was no other way."

He gently patted her still sizzling bottom. "Hopefully repetition will help."

She laughed. "Actually, that reduces the sperm count." She arched her eyes and began to run her fingers up and down his torso. "But that's not really the point, now, is it?" She began to giggle. "The final part of my apology to your mother is to make her a grandmother."

He jumped at the teasing movements. "I guess that 'apology' is the word of the day."

She winked at him. "Actually, I think it is 'Sorry'!"

                THE END

The Great Manifest High School Athletic Caper and The Flippity Uppity Morning

Opening Chapter – Busted!

It was a hot Texas Saturday morning. A number of people were on their way to the modest brick house on the outskirts of Manifest, Texas, the residence of the local school principal, Bart Henderson.

It was a home that Bart Henderson shared with no one else, although he could have changed that circumstance on many an occasion. At forty-eight, the strikingly handsome and long widowed educator had no lack of attention from attractive and eligible women.

He simply was still looking for the right one to share his modest home and quite successful life with. It would take someone special to ever fill his heart the way the young woman with the undetected brain aneurism had.

One such person was in route to his home at that very moment, although she was uncertain as to why. Of course, as Bart waited for everyone to arrive, he knew exactly what was going on, and in his anxiety he ran his fingers through his salt-and-pepper hair. The situation would have been quite awful under any circumstances, but the fact that Deb Calloway was to be involved in the meeting, threw all kinds of wrenches into his plans.

This was just his second year as principal at the Manifest School District, responsible for all grade levels in the small and sparsely populated territory. But at the beginning of his second year there, Deb, now forty-five, had moved to the district to take a job in accounting for a local, large ranching supply company. Along with her came a very talented and athletic, now seventeen-year-old daughter who immediately became the standout player on the girls' basketball team.

For Deb, it was a homecoming. She was a graduate of Manifest High School and had gone away after graduation to attend a community college while living with an aunt and uncle.

At the age of twenty-seven, she had entered into the only serious relationship of her life. Then came her unintentional pregnancy and the birth of Teresa. Neither she nor her boyfriend desired marriage, but she accepted his request to be involved in Teresa's life, and she saw to it that he was. He had been as responsible as she could have ever hoped for, and contributed greatly both financially and emotionally to her upbringing.

When Deb had taken the job in her hometown, the location did not distance Teresa any further from her now married father than their previous location. And when uncomfortable questions were asked, Deb would respond quite matter-of-factly that she had a wonderful daughter who was a blessing to her, the result of a memorable "fling" that she had never regretted.

Bart Henderson and Deb Calloway had met before school started that most recent year at a welcome party and orientation for new students, not something that Manifest had many of in any given year. But that time there were going to be four new students, and he and Deb had seemed to hit it off right away.

They had gone out for lunch a couple of times, Bart being the cautious type, but as the school term had ended and the summer break was upon them, he and Deb had begun to see each other, and before this particular day they had gone out to dinner or to movies five times, becoming very mutually attracted.

There was definitely a strong emotional and physical yearning building at full steam. But now there was a problem to be confronted, and Deb Calloway was right in the middle of it all.

The first to arrive at his home for the appointed time of the meeting was Brenda Howard. The sixty-year-old real estate agent was a person of many talents. She was vice president of the school board, and due to the fact that she had very advanced computer skills, she volunteered her spare time to overseeing the security of the school district's computer systems and programs.

Three years before, there had been an incident in which a member of the junior class had succeeded in hacking into the school's main computer and altering grades for a member of the boys basketball team who was on the edge of losing eligibility due to his scholastic issues.

Something didn't seem right to the head coach of the team, and when the grade reports came out, he persuaded the former principal to have the player's grades audited. And the plot was brought to an end before any damage was done, save for the student hacker being suspended from school for ten days.

The school administration had done a remarkable job of keeping the details under wraps, but decided that it would not hurt to have an extra keen eye always on the school's computer system, and that was where Brenda Howard came in. But she was good at her job, and had brought something to the attention of Bart Henderson. Now Bart was going to be faced with a professional, as well as personal, challenge.

Even though Bart's home was small, he did set one spare bedroom aside to use as an office. He often laughed to his friends that there was no reason for it other than the fact that he simply wanted to have an office in his home. But on this day, being able to have a meeting in his own house in an office setting was going to be advantageous.

He and Brenda sat and talked in a sober tone for a couple of minutes before the doorbell rang. They both walked to the front door to find that at virtually the same time, all others expected at the gathering had arrived He refrained from kissing Deb in front of the others, as they had kept their budding relationship very private for the time being.

Still, he could not take his eyes off of the strikingly and enchanting woman with a mischievous smile and gleaming eyes as she stood there in a little black dress that very much met his approval. Of course, he could have appreciated it more under other circumstances, and he could tell by Deb's expression that she was concerned by the secrecy of the meeting that had been called.

The next to enter was the high school girls' basketball team coach. Emily Metcalf had been named the coach the year before when most people her age were still being appointed to be assistant coaches.

But she, as well as Deb, were alumni of Manifest High School. Emily's own exploits as a member of the high school girls' basketball team there had furthered her consideration to be named to the head coach position after serving as an assistant for three years in a neighboring district.

Emily also was a quite pretty woman, and the beauty with dark brown shoulder length hair had been the homecoming queen at Manifest twelve years earlier. Her figure had not changed a bit, and she and her husband Larry Metcalf, w an attorney in the town of Manifest, certainly made for an eye-catching couple.

Bart decided to not even attempt to put on an air of being happy to see everyone. He just simply went so far as to thank them all for being prompt, and asking them to accompany him to his office.

There was something about him taking a seat behind his desk that gave the mystery meeting an air of seriousness. Among the four people now sitting in guest chairs across the desk from him, only Brenda Howard possessed information about why the meeting had been called, information she wished that she had not possessed.

Bart had trouble forcing out his words at first. "It seems that... I suppose... I need to tell you about a problem that we have discovered. Now you may or may not know that Mrs. Howard here is not only the vice president of our school board, but she also is an authority on computer and data security, and she has served for almost a year and a half, volunteering to keep an eye on our computer system. Most of all, she has been trying to guard against hacks and unauthorized entry into our system."

Suddenly, two stomachs clenched in anxiety as Bart continued. "So now, I'm going to ask Mrs. Howard to explain to you what she recently discovered." Now two stomachs felt as if they were churning.

Brenda Howard cleared her throat and began. "A couple of weeks ago, a special hacking detection program that I installed on our system alerted me to some suspicious activity." Her eyes rose and scanned those sitting to her left, and two of them present began to squirm in their chairs.

"I found a significant, attempted but unsuccessful breach of our system. This was a foiled attempt to block communications from the athletic department at Hirschfeld Falls High School. An attempt was made to block the mechanism through which the various schools sign off on agreements to schedule out of conference athletic meets.

"I tracked this attempt to what appears, almost beyond any question of doubt, to be the computer of our girls' basketball coach, Emily Metcalf." Suddenly, Emily was wiping tears from her eyes, and her attorney husband was turned toward her, stunned by what he was hearing.

"I went on to examine email messages generated around that time on school computers, something that the Board of Education has oversight authority to do. That was when I found an unusual number of emails being exchanged between Mrs. Metcalf and the parent of one of her players. I would like to emphasize that this is not a common practice."

Now Deb Calloway was having a hard time keeping her composure, and that was not unnoticed by anyone else in the room. Brenda Howard continued: "As you may suspect by the composition of this gathering, that parent is Deb Calloway, mother of star player Teresa Calloway.

"Now as all of you know, Hirschfeld Hills is expected to once again have an almost unbeatable girls' high school basketball team this year. And that exchange of emails between the two women to my left made numerous references to the fact that the game against Hirschfeld Hills could be the only thing that would keep the Manifest girls' team from having a possibly undefeated season of their own.

"And I add this to the conversation with reluctance... Mrs. Calloway made two references to how playing for an undefeated team could enhance Teresa's prospects for recruitment by any number of prominent college women's basketball program.

"What is most important for all of you to hear, is that there is no evidence that Teresa had any knowledge of an attempt to prevent what would be two premiere high school girl' teams from playing each other."

The school board vice president stood and walked around to the back of the desk to stand next to where Bart sat. "I can hardly put into words the ramifications that a situation like this can have. Although, I will note that the actions that the two of you attempted to take do not rise to the level of criminal actions.

"I know that because I spoke in the highest confidence to the school board attorney about this." Now the two women involved in the scheme slid down slightly in their chairs as Brenda continued. "At the same time, I would say with great confidence that some of us were put in some peril in legal terms by our decision to handle this on a, let's say, informal basis.

"I know that we have skirted around the laws requiring public access to meetings involving school board officials. I have spoken with a handful of critical board members about this, those who I unreservedly trust to keep things in confidence. The law does really not allow for that kind of maneuvering."

She peered disapprovingly at Deb Calloway and Emily Metcalf for a moment. "As for you, Emily, if this were to be made public, you would likely be disqualified for a number of years from coaching.

"And Mrs. Calloway, if this were to have become public knowledge, it would've been very unfair to your innocent daughter. It may not be fair, but college athletic recruiters would have some reservations about Teresa. You have also risked being seen as attempting to improperly influence public school business and the duties of publicly paid staff. That is where the question of criminal intent becomes murky.

"So, this leaves us with a quandary. What you did is quite serious in intent, and had you succeeded in carrying it out, it would have given our school district a black eye."

Deb began to speak slowly. "Emily and I ran into each other at the library, and we started talking about Teresa and the team and all the possibilities. Then we started doing some wishful 'what if' fantasizing about what it would be like if our school had a clear shot straight to an undefeated season?

"I guess things kind of went downhill from there."

Emily spoke up next. "Deb has described it exactly as I would. It seemed harmless at the time, just talking about at all, but I guess we found ourselves unwilling to dispose of the idea. That was where our judgment failed."

The school board vice president nodded to signal her understanding. "But you did go too far, as both of you seem to acknowledge. Due to the fact that this is not being handled formally through standard procedures and legal processes, those of us who have been discussing what happened have been left with the task of coming up with some manner in which the two of you must pay a penalty for what cannot be described as anything but misbehavior on your part."

The older woman could barely contain herself when she saw the expression on Larry Metcalf's face as he glowered at Emily. "So those of us who discussed the matter came up with what we think is a very fitting manner in which to deal with your failed plot. So I want you to know that but we are offering the two of you as an alternative to having the community know about this. What we are about to relate to you as our chosen course of action, was agreed upon by three other school board members who were consulted, along with myself, and we presented this course of action to Mr. Henderson, here, to implement."

She scanned Emily and Deb with a steely glare before she spoke once again. "And now, Mr. Henderson is about to explain to you what he has been instructed by Board of Education members to carry out as an alternative to making your actions known to the public or state education authorities. Mr. Henderson, if you will."

Bart stood with his hands on his hips, his disappointment evident in his expression, especially when his eyes met those of Deb, the woman he has been hoping to establish a permanent relationship with. He sighed deeply, obviously having a difficult time getting his thoughts together.

"I have been the principal here for now two years, having taken the reins from a revered educator, Mason Powell. Emily... Deb... I know the both of you were students here when he was your principal.

"It was my privilege and pleasure to get to know Mason when I was serving as the assistant principal at Benton Mills Grove. Whenever we were at a conference, I always sought out his advice and counsel.

"And of course, many people who knew him well spoke to me about the manner in which he not only ensured that students at Manifest received the best possible education that a small district like this one could offer, he was also well known for keeping the students here in line in terms of behavior and discipline."

He looked at the two uncomfortable women, fifteen years apart in age, but obviously sharing a common angst in wondering where this lecture was going. "I have heard a lot of stories about what happened with students here who stepped over the line. I have tried to carry on that tradition."

He allowed a wide smile as he stepped around to the front of the desk and sat upon it, finding so much enjoyment in the looks of terror on the faces of his lady friend and his girls basketball coach that he almost felt guilty. Almost.

"Did either of you ladies ever have the pleasure of coming to the school office when Mason Powell was the principal and having that legendary paddle of his land across your tender backsides several times?"

The two women looked at each other nervously, then both looked back at Bert and shook their heads in the negative. He leaned closer to them. "And why not?"

Deb spoke first. "I was... I was afraid to misbehave in school, because I was afraid of getting a paddling from him."

Emily nervously spoke an agreement. "Same here. I had always heard awful stories about that paddle, the one with all the holes in it to make it sting more." Bart could see that she was tearing up as she spoke.

He leaned back and allowed a smile. "Well, ladies, that paddle is still at the school in a closet. But I'm afraid that it is going to see some use once again."

Now Deb and Emily were looking at each other with shocked expressions, while Emily's husband Larry sat looking at them with a look of satisfaction.

"I have to go to a conference for a few days. I will be back next Saturday. Emily… I want you here at 9:00 A.M. sharp that morning. And Larry, you are more than welcome to sit outside my office to listen while business regarding Emily is taking care of in here.

"And Deb… I will address your role in this fiasco one hour later at 10:00.

"I will have that fabled paddle here, and each of you will bend across this very desk and have the privilege of experiencing six times why the school board told me when I took the job to use another paddle, one that would not sting quite so much." He looked again at the two women who were both cringing.

"And as soon as we are finished with your paddling, you're going to go across my knees and receive one very long and hard spanking with my hand."

Now two women looked at each other with their jaws hanging open, but neither of them was about to begin arguing. Each was now very far into a mode of regret, and neither was about to try to make a case that what they were going to be facing was unfair. And that was when Brenda Howard spoke once again.

"I will be present for each and every whack, in keeping with school policy that all corporal punishment be witnessed. And by the way, girls, be sure to wear a dress or a skirt, something quite flippity-uppity."

Emily nearly stuttered. "Uhm...by that you don't mean... I guess you do mean that, don't you?"

Brenda nodded her head. "Yes, that's exactly what I mean. So, I would suggest that for a number of reasons, each of you wear something in the manner of what we usually call granny panties.

"We want you to get the full benefit of what that paddle and Mr. Henderson's hand has to offer, and we certainly wouldn't want the presence of a needless, extra layer of fabric to keep you from getting the full experience intended for you."

Bart scanned the faces of his visitors. "Any questions? Any comments?"

The pink faced Emily turned toward her husband. "You've been awfully quiet."

Her attorney husband Larry shrugged. "So far, I haven't heard anything said that I would disagree with. In fact, I think I'm going to look forward to sitting out here and listening while you tan Emily's hide."

Emily groaned dramatically and shook her head. "You can be so supportive."

Suddenly Larry spoke again. "Now, Mr. Henderson, hasn't it long been a tradition of families around here that if you get paddled by the principal, when you get home to get another good butt warming?"

Now Emily groaned even louder than before as Bart responded. "I certainly would not discourage that, Larry." He turned to look at

Deb. "Why I may even find myself serving as a stand-in father figure for someone else we know next Saturday morning."

There was something in the way that she nearly smiled in response that seemed to go straight to his heart. And then with a gesture of his hand, he indicated that the meeting was over, although Deb remained in her chair until everyone else had left. And when there was only herself and Bart in the office, she got up and lifted herself up on her tiptoes and sat down on the desk next to him, tears beginning to run down her face.

He reached behind to a box of tissues, pulled out a couple and began to dab at her face. A moment later she shook her head and looked down. "I am so sorry, Bart. I'll understand if you no longer want to have a relationship with me... I mean, after you give me what I have coming next Saturday morning."

She looked up and saw that he was shaking his head. "Okay, that was a pretty big screwup. And to be real honest with you, sweetheart, I am shocked that you ever could have gotten started with such a lame brained idea. But I still care for you. I care for you no less today than I did two weeks ago."

She closed her eyes and bit down on her lip and started crying even harder. "Are you sure? I'm a forty-five-year-old woman who tried to do something very childish. I'm really embarrassed and ashamed."

She leaned her head against his shoulder and continued to cry, and even under the circumstances, he was under the spell of her quietly beautiful face, the way her silver streaked hair dusted her shoulders, the way that her shapely legs stuck out from beneath the short blue summer dress.

He put his arm around her and squeezed her tightly, and she turned and put her head on his chest and began to sob. "Whatever evil genius came up with the idea of giving us one grand butt warming certainly got it right."

He nodded his head. "I have to agree... You two deserve to have your bottoms set on fire, and that's exactly what I'm going to do next Saturday morning right here in this office."

Deb sighed deeply. "I can't think of anything that Emily and I deserve any more than that." She laughed softly for a moment. "I swear, I wish that you had that paddle here right now so you could give me a good dose of it in addition to what I have coming next Saturday."

Bart gave her another squeeze. "I think you actually mean that."

She looked at him and laughed once again as she continued to cry. "I meant every word of it."

Bart cleared his throat. "Actually, I brought it home with me today. And if you meant what you just said, then I'm going to pull you over my knee right now, pull up that cute dress and see to it that you sleep on your stomach tonight."

The expression on her face was almost one of relief. "I think I would love it if you would do that. I can't think of anything better that could happen to me right now."

He stood up, and she slid off the desk and stood nearby, her heart racing and her stomach churning as he took several steps to where a briefcase rested next to the wall. She watched in frightened fascination as he placed the briefcase on the desk, and then flipped the latches.

Slowly and dramatically, he raised the top of the briefcase, revealing the decades-old, sting-inducing board handcrafted to bring maximum discomfort to a backside. He picked it up from inside the briefcase, shoved the case away and sat down again on the edge of the desk.

Deb simply stood in front of him for a moment, looking intently at the well used instrument of discipline, three rows of dime sized holes completing its appearance of something to be avoided.

And then, he put the paddle aside and reached for her upper arm and guided her across his left knee. His right foot was still resting on the floor to give him leverage. Deb found her upper torso resting on the surface of the desk, her bottom raised up and vulnerable, and her feet dangling several inches above the floor.

Although he had never before seen her panty covered bottom before, when he shuffled her dress up to her back, Deb was not at all embarrassed in his seeing her white nylon undies stretching in front of him to contain her curvy bottom. She felt him turn slightly to take hold of the paddle he had placed on the desk, then she felt it being tapped across her upturned backside as Bart tightly gripped the board just above the handle

There was no warning. He simply brought the paddle down energetically enough to generate a loud and quite painful... WHACK... Deb absorbing the shock of the first impact of the paddle in silence.

Deb was full of remorse. She did not want him to do anything other than what he was doing... Bart was cracking the paddle across her thinly covered bottom powerfully and rapidly. She could barely catch her breath between the paddle's fiery landings across her soft, sensitive sit spot that was quickly beginning to feel as if it were engulfed in flames.

These were surreal sensations to Deb. But in her emotional state at that moment, if given the choice she would have preferred a more intense paddling to one less painful.

She surprised herself at the manner in which she was content to simply be there across his knee, willfully, even thankfully, accepting the repeated, fiery sting. Each time the paddle landed, it did so more painfully than the one before, the heat and soreness in her bottom ramping up the effect of each forceful smack.

It was a confusing seven minute long episode. She was crying some from the pain of course, but at least as many of the tears were due to her self recrimination and embarrassment.

But the rest came from her emotional reaction to realizing that what was happening to her at that moment was making her feel closer than ever before to the man vigorously slamming the paddle across her flaming bottom. And that was comforting.

She, like the man paddling her, was long single, but at least she had Teresa as a result of that one union. But she found it to be a confusing acknowledgment that being paddled by this man she cared so much for was in its own way the most intimate experience of her life.

Each time the paddle arrived with its fiery impact, she began to fear the next one to arrive. And at the same time, each time she felt the sting radiate out from the area of the strike, she also felt the warmth radiate and bloom across her bottom, even below the surface. She was also transfixed by the manner in which the sensations were seeming to travel to and stimulate all parts of the middle of her body, making the next painful whack of the paddle something she was both fearing and yearning to feel.

He stopped when she had stoically and bravely absorbed the thirty-fifth whack, although she was aware that when she was bent across the desk and he was having a full range of motion at his disposal, the paddle would be landing with much more fire and fury. But she assured herself that she would handle that moment in the same manner, although she did cringe in remembering that the school board vice president would be witnessing the events of that morning.

She knew it would be quite scary to go through. But that did not mean that she had not just endured a long and painful paddle spanking in relative silence. She had dabbed at her eyes with tissues while it was taking place, but she had never cried out or begged for it to be over.

Rather, when she was again standing, although her knees felt weak, she simply laid her head against his chest and cried softly as he held her tightly, leaning down from time to time to kiss the top of her head.

He led her into the living room, and he sat down at one end of the sofa, while she stretched out upon it and rested her head on his lap as the soft crying continued. Finally' she looked up at him, her lip quivering. "I think I'm crying more because I feel so badly about what happened, more than because I just got that very much-deserved paddling."

He began to run his fingers through her hair and responded to her in a soft voice. "It only matters that you need to know that you can always lay your head on my lap if you need to cry, regardless of the reason.

"I just want you to know that I'm not going to let go of you for one mistake." He continued to stroke her hair for a moment. "But oh, next Saturday morning, I am going to spank your ass so hard and so long...".

In spite of the pain she was in and the emotional distress she was experiencing, she looked up at him and began to giggle at the way he had said that. And at the same time, it brought her comfort in a strange way, hearing him say such a thing to her.

She remained at his home for the rest of the day and far into the evening. By early evening she was able to sit down in relative comfort once again to enjoy the dinner he had prepared on the grill.

But all day, they talked about what had brought about the events of that day.

He finally felt that she was truly convinced that he meant it when he told her that he was already developing such strong feelings for her it would take much more than the recent happenings to make him not want to be with her. Each time that was said, she broke down and cried in happiness.

Many times during that day and evening, they found themselves suddenly embracing tightly and kissing. The irony was not lost on them that a major crisis in their relationship was making that relationship more solid as the day went on, with more reason to hope that it was indeed going to be the relationship both have been looking for, and for quite some time.

~~~

For Emily and Larry, their day had been equally interesting after they had left Bart's house. Larry was a kind and understanding man, and in his work as an attorney had become privy to many an interesting marital situation. But this was his marriage that was undergoing a quite unique trauma.

Emily's feelings were very similar to those Deb had been coping with since their failed but nonetheless attempted plot had been revealed to have been uncovered.

The first mile of their drive home from Bart's house was accomplished in total, frozen silence. Finally, Larry spoke in a stern, slow cadence: "You know, Emily... I love you more today than the day we were married six years ago.

"But right now, I feel like what you need is for me to take you across my knees for a spanking that would go on for a long, long time."

She finally broke her own silence. "It scares me to have to admit that I'm thinking the same thing." Larry thought that he could actually hear her gulp before she continued. "I think that bedtime this evening would be a good time for that."

She reached for her purse and pulled out her phone and tapped a couple of times. "Hey, Mom. I got your text this morning... I'm sure that little Carrie would love that too. Sure that you're ready for our little four-year-old bundle of energy?... Okay, I'll bring her over right after lunch."

She tapped her phone once again and put it back in her purse. When she turned to look at him, he detected a hint of a smile. "Now we won't have to worry about our little munchkin happening upon seeing Mommy getting her bare bottom paddled a deep dark red with that wooden hairbrush I keep in the bathroom."

She looked at him again and shrugged. "I guess you can tell that even before we left the boss's house, I was kind of planning out our evening."

He reached over and patted her on her knee. "I'm proud of you for that."

She sighed loudly. "The spanking I'm getting tonight... I'm really okay with that. I appreciate your saying that you're proud of me for being so accepting of it, but I'm not feeling very proud of myself right now. So I guess that's part of why I am feeling strangely anxious for it to take place."

She sighed and leaned her head back. "And our little daughter is going to feel so spoiled. Her favorite babysitter in the morning, and going to spend the night at Grandma's house."

He reached over and patted her on the knee once again. "Well, if you feel like it after I give your butt a good working over tonight, maybe I can do something to spoil you, too."

She looked back at him with one arched eye. "I'm not exactly certain that those two things go hand-in-hand, but I suppose we can find out."

~~~

As the emotionally exhausted and tender – bottomed Deb was kissing the Principal of the Manifest School District good night before walking to her car, two miles away Emily was getting out of the tub full of scented bubbles to get ready for the rest of the memorable evening.

Of course, all that she had to do to get ready for what was to take place next was to simply slide one of Larry's T-shirts over her head. That being done, she stared for a moment at the large wooden hairbrush on the bathroom counter, picked it up and walked out into the bedroom.

Her husband was sitting on the edge of the bed, patting the space to his right to indicate where he wanted her to sit. She walked slowly, handed him the hairbrush and sat down.

Larry leaned toward her and kissed her. "Are you scared?"

She nodded her head, but smiled at the same time. "I always have been right before a spanking."

He patted her on the knee. "You can remember that far back?"

Her face turned pink and she grimaced: "Well, not as long ago as you might think. I know this is risky under the circumstances, but I have to confess to you that I kind of lied today."

His eyes opened wide and he could not resist allowing a smile. "You lied today about exactly what?"

She shrugged and seemed to bury her head in her shoulders. "Well, it was more that I could have been much more forthcoming. You see, when Saturday morning rolls around, it will not be the first time that that very paddle has landed across my panties."

She could not help but laugh at the expression on her husband's face as she continued. "I was a senior, and of course Mr. Powell was the big guy in charge. And I went through a stage after I turned eighteen where I thought that I should be able to get by with more things at that age.

"Well, one morning in March, myself and three other seniors, all them boys, got sent down to the office because we kept horsing around in study hall. To say the least, Mr. Powell did not approve of that. So, he told us we were all going to get a paddling, and I was really scared.

"The boys went first. I was shaking like a leaf while I waited for my turn. We had to stand in line outside his office door and listen to these really loud, scary whacks. And I could also hear some verbal reactions as one by one, the guys went into the office and got their three whacks and came out looking quite distressed.

"Then it was my turn, and Mr. Powell said what everybody already knew, that everybody had to bend over and touch your toes unless you were a girl wearing a dress or a skirt. Then you just had to bend over and put your hands on your knees. Then you just got either whacked a little harder or got an extra one. Or in my case, both.

"You see, that morning I had put on this very short blue-and-white flowered dress that Mom only let me wear on the weekends, because she thought it was too short to wear to school, regardless of the dress code. Of course, that dress did violate the dress code.

"So that really did not help me much with Mr. Powell. He lectured me for a couple of minutes about breaking the rules on clothing. So then he told me to just bend over and put my hands on my knees, and he was going to give me the additional whack. I was simply terrified.

"So I leaned forward and put my hands on my knees, and I could tell that my dress was just barely covering my bottom, and maybe not even completely. And then, he gave me the first whack, and he was not fooling around.

"I let out a bit of a squeal, because that first one made me start to cry, it stung so bad. Then he gave me the second one, and it landed on the same exact territory.

"He managed to make the third one hit the very same spot and I was really crying. Then I got the last one, and I cried out pretty loud.

"That would have been enough for one day, except during the fourth period math class, right after lunch, some of us got into this silly thing of throwing pennies at each other across the room. And I took part, warm, sore bottom and all. And guess who got caught by the teacher right in the middle of throwing one of the pennies?

"So I was given a note to take to the office, and I knew I was done for. I knew that Mr. Powell was just going to beside himself because we all knew that he had never had someone sent back to the office for misbehavior after already having been paddled that same day. So, legal adult or not, my goose was cooked, and I had a hard time putting one foot in front of the other to go back to the office with that note.

"The man was livid! He told me to go outside his office and have a seat, that he was going to call my mother. Of course, I knew that was not going to go well for me. So, it turns out that they had a very interesting conversation.

"A few minutes later, he opens his door and asked the secretary to come in. And about a minute later, she is standing with a rather threatening smirk on her face as she told me to come back in.

"I had to stand there and listen to him give a summary of his conversation with Mom. It seems that they had discussed not only my behavior and my paddling that morning, but my wearing of the forbidden dress as well.

"As it turns out, Mom told him to go ahead and paddle me again, and this time to make me bend over and touch my toes so that he would be sure to give me a good working over right where I sat down. And he added that Mom told him that if I found the results of bending over in that forbidden dress embarrassing, then all the better.

"And just when I was standing there quaking with fear, and wondering how it could get any worse, he told me that I was going to get five whacks this time. And when he told me that, I started crying.

"But there was no mercy for this girl on that day. He just grabbed his paddle and put his hand on my back and guided me over to where the condemned bent over and waited. Then he puts his hand on my back between my shoulder blades and starts to press me down, and he did that until I was touching the ends of my sandals.

"Of course, I could feel that the hem of my dress was now far above his target area, and that was when I remembered I had put on these white panties with little pink hearts all over them. Then I had this irrational joke flash through my mind, wondering how many hearts were going to be broken by the time my paddling was over.

"I bent over, my panties on full display, and he started to tap that paddle against me. and shuffle it back and forth to take aim. I could feel those holes, and I remembered from my first paddling of the day just how much that thing had stung through my dress.

"And then a couple of seconds later I found out that even having that thin dress missing made a difference all I could do was clench my teeth to keep from crying like a baby as he put all he had into each and every one of those whacks.

"The funny thing is, here I am sitting next to you, my handsome hunk lawyer husband who is about to paddle my bare ass, and I'm feeling the same thoughts that I felt during that paddling. I had no one to blame but myself, and the sooner I took my lickin' like a big girl, the better off I would be.

"You see, I remember that when I was a kid, I hardly ever got spanked. All I needed was for my father to threaten to give me what he referred to as…a darned good lickin'. I never wanted to find out just how darned good he may have been at giving a spanking.

"But now, my breathtakingly adorable man, I'm ready to take what I have coming to me."

Larry tapped the hairbrush across his chin several times, pretending to be in deep and consequential thought: "I once again want to say that I admire you for your attitude toward all this.

"But now I think I have to decide how to make this an extremely effective experience for you."

Emily put her hands to her face and groaned theatrically. "You are an evil, sadistic genius. I'm certain you will come up with some way to make this an event I will never forget."

He thought for another second, then arched his eyes and grinned as he grasped her upper left arm. "I think that perhaps unpredictability may just make this a more beneficial exercise for you." As he was speaking, he was turning slightly to his left and pulling Emily across his knees, allowing the upper half of her body to rest on the bed.

"I think that you will benefit from my seeing to it that every smack of the hairbrush stings like crazy." Then he shuffled the T-shirt up onto the middle of her back, leaving her bare from the middle of her back on down.

"But then, some of them are going to be much harder, and I think it will be good for you to not know when one like that is on its way."

And before she had a chance to respond, he brought the hairbrush down on her bare bottom with a sharp... SMACK!

"So you and Deb thought that you could get away with singling out one particular school to not end up on your schedule." SMACK... SMACK... SMACK... WHAM! A high-pitched squeal filled the room as a dark pink impression of the hairbrush bloomed across her right bottom cheek.

"And you were willing to inconvenience the staff at another school in the process." SMACK... SMACK... WHAM... WHAM... WHAM! That volley was accompanied by a series of desperate yelps.

"You violated school district policy use of publicly owned computers." SMACK... SMACK... SMACK... SMACK... SMACK... SMACK... SMACK... SMACK! Now Emily was squirming, but she was not in any way trying to resist receiving her paddling.

"And you put that girl Teresa's recruitment efforts in a difficult position." WHAM... WHAM... WHAM... WHAM... WHAM. Another series of squeals filled the bedroom, but not a single word of protest or request for the paddling to either come to an and or lightened in its severity.

"You put the school district's data processing security at risk." SMACK... SMACK... SMACK.

"But most of all...". SMACK... SMACK... SMACK... SMACK... SMACK. "Most of all, you are a role model to the students." WHAM... WHAM... WHAM... WHAM... WHAM... WHAM. Now the sniffling and soft sobbing was constant. SMACK... SMACK... SMACK... SMACK... SMACK... SMACK... SMACK.

"You put your career in jeopardy." WHAM... WHAM... WHAM... WHAM... WHAM. And then she suddenly found herself being pulled up to sit on his lap. She didn't mind the discomfort of that at all as she was held tightly and securely.

"Don't you ever do anything like this again, or I swear I'm going to ask Bart if I can have that paddle to keep here in our house."

In spite of the pain, in spite of the emotions, in spite of the fact that her head was buried against his chest, she managed a soft laugh: "it may come in handy from time to time."

They laid down on the bed after Larry turned back the covers, and he reached to the bedside stand to turn off the only light that was on in the room. He again pulled her into his arms and held her tightly as he stroked her back and kissed her.

Finally a soft voice, but obviously one full of anxiety began to speak in a near whisper. "Larry, sweetie... I want to thank you for paddling me just like I deserved."

He placed a kiss on her forehead. "I don't know if this will reassure you or scare you, but I thought it would be harder for me to do that than it was." He was relieved when she responded with quiet laughter interspersed with the sniffling and wiping away tears.

"Sweetie... I'm afraid that I have one more thing to confess to you, something I've never told anyone, but now I think the time is right."

He pulled the covers over them to keep her warm. "Go ahead and tell me. You don't ever have to keep any secrets from me."

Even in the diminished light, he could see that her face had turned dark pink. "Okay, here goes.

"That day I got those paddlings from Mr. Powell... I guess we're talking twelve years ago. The night after that happened, I felt really exhausted and I went to bed early that evening.

"I couldn't get to sleep because I kept reliving those paddlings in detail. The problem was, Larry.... The memories got me all... turned on.

"So today, when the boss told Deb and I what we were in for, the whole thing just struck me as ironic. But when you made that comment about how you thought that you should spank me at home as well, the thought of that just… Oh, wow!"

Larry continued to stroke her back. "So that paddling I just gave you…?"

Emily laughed softly and nodded her head. "I… am… so… turned on right now. I can't really understand why, but I sure am."

He gave her a hard deep kiss. "So do you have any special requests in terms of alleviating that condition within your strawberry bubble scented body?"

She fluttered her lashes. "Well, we both know what gives me the most intense climax, and considering how horny I am right now, I think that I could enjoy getting another good lickin' right now." She giggled and leaned forward and kissed him, her face a dark pink. "But not the same kind of lickin' this time."

She gasped in anticipation as he began to suckle at her nipples, then began to work his way down her chest and then to her abdomen. "All right, young lady, if you think that you need a good lickin', a good lickin' you're going to get"

~~~.

Deb lay in her bed in her rented condo in the only recently built housing unit in Manifest. She thought back to when she had encountered Teresa that evening and could hardly look her straight in the eyes. She shook her head as she considered how she had attempted such a misguided effort on behalf of an offspring anyone could imagine.

She felt so disappointed in herself, she considered the best part of the day to have been when she had found herself across Bart's knee as he paddled the daylights out of her. She knew that was appropriate and necessary.

Her greatest relief was that Bart still cared for and wanted her in spite of what she had done. And at that moment, she would have given anything to have him with her in that lonely bed, even making love to him for the first time. She was wondering how long she could wait for that to take place.

At the same time, two miles away, Bart was restless. Although he should have been tired and sleepy from nothing more than the stress of the day, he found himself staring at the living room window for no particular reason.

He had been rattled to the core to find out that this woman he had come to care for so deeply could have been involved in such a reckless effort. At the same time, he had been taken with how genuinely apologetic she had been, and the manner in which she actually welcomed going across his knee to have her bottom soundly and extensively paddled.

Everything could have been avoided with a little more forethought, or just time to reconsider actions. But there was one particular point in the whole complex issue that made it impossible for him to walk away from Deb. And that factor was simply the reality that he was now in love with her.

~~~

Emily and Larry lay in a naked embrace beneath the covers as she giggled and tapped him on the lips. "Best damned lickin' you've ever given me. And you have given me some that were simply unreal."

He arched his eyes and growled appreciatively. "And I very much enjoyed how expertly you treated me to the male version of what I did to you."

He shook his head and laughed. "Life can be funny like that. One minute I'm paddling the fanny of the most beautiful woman I have ever met, and the next thing I know I'm being blown to bits."

He ran his hand across her cheek as both of them dissolved into laughter. "Now what am I going to do? If we ever decide that you need spanked again for misbehaving… I'm not going to know if I'm actually punishing you." They both began to laugh as they embraced once again.

"Don't worry, my man, because even if it turns me on, it sure still hurts like hell." She sighed deeply. "And next Saturday morning is not going to be any treat for me. I already know from experience that one hard spanking followed by another in the same day is one thing.

"But next Saturday, the boss is going to paddle me and then immediately take me across his knees for a long hard spanking. There's not going to be a few hours between them for my butt to have a chance to cool down.

"At the same time, I understand that that's the whole point of the boss doing it that way. That paddling is going to be hot enough. And then the spanking right after… I guess it just makes that spanking more deservedly painful. And that is just what Deb and I both deserve."

Now she felt a bit of unease as she saw how Larry was looking at her through narrowed eyes. "Okay, my devious man, what are you thinking about?"

He shrugged and displayed his evil grin. "Oh, you just reminded me of something I had been thinking of during the past day. I take it that you would not find any disagreement in my suggesting that when it's time for us to head toward Bart's house, that you arrive with your bottom already quite warm and buzzing, so that you indeed allow yourself to return home that morning one very thoroughly spanked, and gorgeous woman."

She looked at him suspiciously. "I thought you said something about getting it at home… after… getting paddled by the principal."

He nodded his head slowly: "The one prior does not need to exclude the one after."

She shook her head and laughed. "I hope you understand just how rotten you are. But right is right, my man. What I tried to do is deplorable." Then she snuggled up close to him, and that was the way they woke in the morning.

~~~

It was Wednesday evening when Bart called Deb after his last seminar, only two days remaining during his conference before he could return home to the many issues facing him. "I'm still so sorry, Bart about what we did…about what I did.

"It seemed at the beginning that we were just teasing each other about such a scheme. And then it seemed to take on a life of its own, and the next thing we knew it didn't sound as serious as it really was. I don't know if either one of us can say whether we really would have gone through with it, but we both understand that we put so much in jeopardy by even taking those initial steps to see what could possibly be put into motion."

Bart remained silent for a moment: "Deb, I just know that this is out of character for you, and I know that it's out of character for Emily as well. I just want for us to deal with this and put it behind us. No pun intended."

He heard Deb laughing. "Very aptly phrased, Bart. But I think that the most important thing when this coming Saturday morning is over, is that none of us walk away feeling that this egregious lapse in judgment has not been dealt with as harshly as needed."

Chapter 2

The Flippity Uppity Morning

It was a Saturday morning that dawned with several people feeling anxious for a common reason, although their roles in the events to unfold were quite distinct from each others'.

For Bart, he was going to be administering extensive and painful corporal punishment to two women he would prefered to have never had reason to as much as verbally chastise. All in all, he was feeling sadness more than anything else.

As for Mrs. Howard, she was going to be observing the punishments that she had a central role in suggesting. She liked both of the women who were going to spend the day unable to sit down, but she had little sympathy for the manner in which they had gotten themselves into such a predicament.

Of course, for Deb, she was still struggling with the angst of having to accept her own lapse into moral failure, even if she had wanted to help her daughter. She was thankful that her plot had failed, and her daughter would never have to know the manner in which her mother had slipped.

And of course, as for the co-conspirator, Emily, the day was going to be especially memorable for her. She glanced at her watch as she made the finishing touches on being ready for what promised to be a rather miserable morning. She saw that she and Larry would be leaving their own house in forty-five minutes for the fifteen minute drive to the residence of her principal.

And there was some dramatic action about to take place before that departure. But through it all, she smiled at the memory of the grin on her mother's face the evening before at having her granddaughter dropped off for yet another quite welcome overnight visit.

For Emily's husband Larry, it was an unusual morning, but not really something he was dreading at all. As much as he deeply loved Emily, there had simply been no excuse for what she had tried to accomplish. The fact that she had jeopardized a budding career she loved only added to the folly of it all.

He glanced at the clock to see that it was just about time for him to begin the process of getting Emily's day off to a most deservedly painful start. And she understood and even agreed when he had explained to her that he was going to be sitting outside Bart's home office listening to some very interesting sounds that he hoped would be quite distinct and dramatic.

~~~

There had been only one change of plans. Bart had woken at 5:30 after a restless night, only to glance at his phone to see that he had received a text from Deb just before he had been roused from his minimal slumber. He called her, and he then agreed that he would pick her up and bring her to his house. She would make herself scarce in the spare bedroom in the back of the small dwelling while justice was applied to Emily's backside.

When he picked her up, he was relieved that she did not seem the least bit nervous. In fact, she explained to him along the way that she felt very much at peace that morning with how the issue was being resolved.

In spite of the emotions of the morning, Bart's spirits were simply lifted by being with Deb. He certainly did not mind the company of a beautiful woman he had come to love. Even though it was in accordance with the instructions that had been given, he very much appreciated the view of her sitting there in the car in the short and silky beige dress.

When they got to the house, she looked at her watch, straightened her posture, and then took a deep breath. "I'm going to disappear now." She surprised even herself with a quiet laugh. "I may put cotton in my ears while you're painting Emily's bottom several shades of red." Then they leaned together and kissed, and she turned quickly and walked to the back of the house to await her turn bending over the desk and then laying across Bart's knees.

The next to arrive was Brenda Howard. She seemed more subdued than Bart would have expected, but she strived to be businesslike as she chatted with him and went over the few details necessary. And then, at 8:50, another car arrived and Emily and Larry were met at the door by Bart and Brenda.

Bart did not think that it was his imagination that Emily seemed not only anxious as would be expected, but also coping with some discomfort. Then they all walked into the office, Bart and school board vice president Brenda, along with Emily and Larry.

It was hard for Emily to avert her gaze from the paddle that was already present on the desk. She may not have seen it for twelve years, but she definitely recalled that one day in which her bottom and that board were in frequent contact.

Everyone went silent, so Bart spoke: "I appreciate that you came along Larry. When we get ready to begin, you can just make yourself comfortable in that stuffed chair right outside the door, unless you want to be a little more distant from the sounds."

Larry shook his hand and smiled. "Thank you Mr. Henderson, but Emily knows that I will be right outside, although she also knows that I am enthusiastically supportive of how this is being handled." He put his arm on Emily's shoulder. "And please be assured that I am doing all that I can to play an active role in seeing to it that Emily fully comprehends the seriousness of this matter."

Emily took a deep breath, her face turning pink. "And I promised to Larry that I would verify to you that he is indeed doing his part. As a matter of fact, about thirty minutes ago, I received the last whack of a very sound spanking…". She glanced warily at Larry who folded his arms, nodded his head and motioned with his finger for her to continue. "Uhm, a very sound spanking on… my… uhm b…b…bare… bot…bottom."

She grimaced for a moment. "And I'm getting what my husband is referring to as a 'Just to make sure' spanking after we get home." She sighed deeply. "I think I covered everything I was supposed to report on."

Brenda Howard stepped toward Emily and put her hand on her shoulder. "And thank you for dressing in accordance with our instructions."

Emily reached down and gave the short, blue pleated dress with white polka dots a bit of a twirl. "Thank you, I thought it would be appropriate."

Emily's face turned pink once again and she looked at her husband with a comical scowl. "And by the way, once we get underway, you will have the opportunity to admire something that my amazing husband ordered off the Internet specifically for the events of this morning." In spite of the tension, everyone there had difficulty suppressing laughter.

Bart cleared his throat, and tried to assume a more businesslike demeanor, something that matched the seriousness of the Navy blue suit he was wearing, complete with white shirt and an austere black tie.

"Okay, Emily just to make sure that you understand completely what's going to happen... I'm going to have you bend over the desk, I will then raise your dress up onto your back.

"I will give you six swats with the paddle, each of them roughly ten seconds apart. I want to warn you, they're going to be hard, and the sting from the paddle is going to be perhaps overwhelming.

"Immediately when you have received the sixth and final swat, without delay and without any regard to the pain you are feeling, I'm going to sit down on one of these chairs and you will lower yourself across my knees.

"I will then administer a very long and hard spanking. You will not be given any hint as to how many smacks of my hand you will receive. Part of the punishment aspect of the spanking will be the fact that you will have no idea as to when it will end.

"Now Emily, would you prefer to instead be subjected to administrative discipline within the school system and the athletic organizations overseeing your position?"

Emily immediately shook her head back and forth. "No, I'm going to do this."

Bart seemed to freeze in anxiety for a moment, then took a deep breath and turned to Emily's husband Larry. "Well then, Mr. Metcalf, feel free like I said to either take a seat right outside the office or, if you prefer, remove yourself from being able to hear Emily's punishment taking place."

Larry stepped over to his wife and put his hands on her shoulders, then kissed her on the lips. "I'll be right outside." He kissed her once again, then stepped through the door and pulled it closed behind him.

Bart took off his suit coat, then rolled up the sleeve of his dress shirt. He then picked up the paddle and gestured toward the desk, and Emily blew out a long breath, and stepped up to the edge of the desk. Her face turned pink as she gathered up the skirt of the short polka dot dress, held it to her waist and bent over the desk

Bart and Brenda had to regain their solemn demeanor at that point, seeing for themselves what special item Larry had ordered for Emily to wear that morning. On a pair of full cut, gleaming white satin panties were emblazoned colorful bull's-eyes on each bottom cheek.

Sensing what was causing the hesitation, Emily sighed in resignation and shook her head as she spoke slowly. "Larry said that you would probably appreciate having this to aim at. I don't think that Larry is as funny as he thinks he is."

Bart dramatically cleared his throat. "I'm certain it will be helpful. Are you ready, Emily?"

Her soft response was barely audible. "I think I'm as ready as I'm going to be."

Bart patted the paddle against the colorful targets several times. "You know I can't take into account that you've already been spanked this morning."

She once again sighed heavily: "That's okay. Bart thought that it would make my paddling hurt even more, because that's what I deserve." She looked back at Bart who was now pressing the paddle against the seat of her panties. "And I can't argue with that. So, I'm ready."

Outside the office, Larry was finding himself a little more tense than he had anticipated feeling, and a little more concerned than he wanted to feel in regard to how well Emily was going to be able to cope with what she was facing.

He began to wonder if he had been too uncaring about her emotions, even though he knew that it was all part of what she had to go through to come out of the situation feeling that she had been sufficiently penalized. Then he was roused from his thoughts by a loud and unnerving... CRACK.

He muttered to himself... "Ouch". He was trying to process just how much that must have hurt just as... CRACK! "Oh, whoa!"

But that was when he started reliving the conversations that had been taken place during the past week. There was talk about everything from harming Teresa Calloway's scholarship quest, to job loss, to even legal jeopardy, and this time when a loud... CRACK...was accompanied by a cry of pain, he steeled himself against the impulse to protect his wife from what even she acknowledged she needed to experience.

Seconds later... CRACK...a muted squeal could barely be heard. The array of hazards Emily and Deb had brought down upon themselves once again at that moment seemed overwhelming... CRACK.

He could hear some muted conversation, although it sounded quite calm and measured. And then... CRACK. It was the sixth and final strike of the paddle. Suddenly, he felt very somber in assuming that she was on the other side of that door crying, still facing much more.

And it didn't take long for that second phase to commence. He doubted that much more than twenty seconds had passed since the last crack of the paddle before... SMACK. Bart's hand had fallen with great energy upon Emily's panty covered bottom.

Just a few seconds later... SMACK. Immediately the spanking had found its rhythm. Every four seconds or so... SMACK... SMACK... SMACK... SMACK... SMACK.

The spanking was steady and relentless... SMACK... SMACK... SMACK... SMACK... SMACK.

Emily was being spanked quite hard, right after a very hard paddling that had been preceded by a not insignificant spanking before leaving home.

It did not take long before every... SMACK... was accompanied by an "Ouch", a squeal, a yelp or simply some unintelligible reaction to the pain. But never was there a plea of any type.

Larry could not help but count... Twenty... Twenty-five... Thirty. The sounds did not indicate that the force behind the spanks had diminished at all... Thirty-five.

But now he could hear Emily crying out each time the hand landed, and there was no question he could hear her sobbing. But her cries and her sobbing, as she had been forewarned, was not a limiting factor in her punishment... SMACK... SMACK... SMACK... Forty... SMACK... SMACK... On and on... Forty-five... Fifty.

Now the only sounds he could hear from inside the room was his wife's sobs interspersed with her apologies for all that had happened. And then, for several minutes there was some muted conversations going on as the sounds of her sobbing began to quiet.

Finally, after what seemed like an eternity to the waiting Larry, the door opened. He stood up and she rushed into his arms. In the background, a somber Bart Henderson looked on, watching as Emily was escorted by her husband to the door.

As soon as it was only Bart and Brenda Howard in the room, she stepped up to him and put her hand on his shoulder. "Need a break?"

He nodded his head. "I feel like I need one, but I need to get the rest of this over with."

She sighed deeply and shook her head. "Bart, if you think that people don't know about you and Deb, you're kidding yourselves."

Bart turned slowly to look at her, his expression one of surprise, but she continued. "Bart, it's one of the reasons we were so compelled to handle this internally. A lot of the board members had gotten to know Deb in the short time since she moved here. And you, Bart, you are beloved.

"And everyone cares very deeply about Emily as well. But you and Deb are kind of looked upon as a special pair, in spite of your feeble attempts to not be noticed together going to dinner and such. You see, Bart, part of everyone's thinking was that they wanted to give the two of you every possible chance.

"And yet, everyone is very upset with what Emily and Deb tried to do. I mean, very upset."

Bart laughed and nodded. "So you're saying...?"

Brenda laughed as well. "What I'm saying is, I think it's time that you go back and fetch that beautiful girlfriend of yours, and see to it that she cannot sit down for a week."

Two minutes later, Bart reentered the office, hand-in-hand with Deb. He wasted no time.

He stepped over to the desk and picked up the paddle. "Any desire to take the more traditional and legal course of action?" He cleared his throat. "And by the way, it turns out we're not a secret."

Deb put her hands behind her back and began to sway gently. "No turning back. I'm all in with this." She stepped closer to him, put her arms around his waist and gave him a kiss on the cheek.

He cleared his throat dramatically: "Ready to be paddled?"

She surprised him by winking at him in response. "Yes, if you think that you're ready to do the paddling."

He cleared his throat once again as he tapped the paddle on the surface of the desk, and he would swear forever that she made "eyes" at him as she stepped toward the desk and bent across it.

It was over quickly, much more quickly than had been the case when Emily had taken her turn across the desk. With a dramatic flair, Bart whisked her dress up onto her back, revealing elegant, beige lace trimmed panties that matched her dress perfectly. But also unlike Emily's turn, once the dress had been dispensed with, he applied a solid smack with his hand that surprised her and caused her to jolt and yelp.

It took only seconds… Six sharp cracks of the paddle delivered with significantly more force than the ones suffered by Emily, a rapid and unyielding paddling that left Deb in tears. And less than ten seconds after she had stood up and began to furiously rub her bottom, she found herself across Bart's knees receiving the first hard smacks of her spanking.

This time, no one was bothering to count, unlike when Emily had found herself across Bart's knees while Brenda Howard secretly clicked a little mechanical counter with each whack. Bart was spanking Deb as if it was his intention to wear away the silky fabric covering her bottom.

Deb was crying hard and more than forty five smacks had been delivered when Bart paused: "Mrs. Howard, if you would be so kind… In the upper left-hand drawer of my desk is a smaller paddle that I found in a closet at the school. I can make exceptionally valuable use of it right now."

He did not think that it was his imagination that Deb gasped as the smaller paddle, this one also with holes, passed in front of her eyes as it was handed to Bart.

Within seconds, Deb knew that the second stage of her spanking was going to be more fiery and painful than the first part. And after fifteen solid smacks with the previously unseen paddle, Bart knew that she would be able to go on from that moment feeling that she had been sufficiently punished.

~~~

By the time Larry pulled into their driveway, Emily was relieved that she could finally spring from the car seat that seemed to have prolonged her spanking during the drive home. Once inside, she turned to Larry with an almost pleading expression: "I'm not trying to stall the inevitable. But I feel grimy and sweaty, like I've just run a marathon, and I would like to take a quick shower."

He caressed her shoulder for a moment. "Go ahead and take a long time. I want to give you some space right now, so I'm going to go ahead and do some calisthenics, then I'll catch a shower in the other bathroom."

As much as she would have liked to have spent an extended period of the cool water running across the back of her, she nonetheless was feeling herself becoming relaxed as she scrubbed her body with the scented body wash, her mind reeling with mixed emotions and confusing urges.

She got out after what seemed an almost endless shower and began patting herself dry with a towel, unable to resist once again turning her back to the full-length mirror and looking at the surreal image of her mottled crimson and white, but mostly crimson, buttocks reflecting back at her. And now she was about to receive more, the final stage of her penalty for having come so close to jeopardizing so much.

She stood naked before the mirror, watching herself slide the wisp of a silky, almost translucent pale green nightie down her body. She took a deep breath, picked up the hairbrush from the counter and walked through the door into the bedroom.

Larry was looking a little too good to her at that moment. Neither of them were going to be going anywhere that day, nor was any company to be expected. So he was sitting there bare chested in his black lounging pants and, leaning against the high headboard of the bed.

He gestured toward the hairbrush: "You can leave that in the bathroom. I want to give you a very personal spanking…the flesh of my hand upon the flesh of your bottom."

She felt a sense of relief when she walked into the bathroom, then returned to stand next to the bed without the painful brush. She crawled onto the bed and knelt next to Larry as he began to run his fingers through her hair.

"I promise you, Larry… I will never give you or anyone else reason to distrust me again."

He smiled warmly as he saw tears begin to run down her cheeks. "I will take your word on that. I believe you. But at the same time, it's important to you and to me that when tomorrow morning rolls around, you can continue on with feeling satisfied that you paid a dear price for your misadventure."

She nodded in agreement, then leaned closer and put her arms around his neck and they kissed. "You know, my hunk, I have some scrambled thoughts right now.

"I feel absolutely convinced that another good butt whacking will be just the right icing on the cake for this unforgettable day. But there's something new going on inside of me that seems to have started with that spanking I got from you when we got home from our meeting with the boss.

"I'm turned on by the thought of you spanking me right now. But I know I'm not going to actually enjoy it while it's taking place.

"But I know that when it's over, I'm going to get all crazy turned on by the sensations. I don't know if I'm abnormal, but I really don't care." They both began to laugh before she continued.

She leaned close again and touched her nose to his, and then treated him to the expression that he knew unfailingly would result in his enjoying some intense physical pleasure within the next half hour…there was that tilt of her head and the arching of her eyes, followed by the fluttering of her lashes.

Then there was the other telltale sign that she was hopelessly aroused, her speaking in a hushed tone: "is this going to be a pretty hard spanking?"

He nodded slowly, straining to keep a matter of fact persona in place: "It's going to be a brief but very hard spanking. Just five, but you're going to wonder if your boss secretly made his way here with his paddle."

She winced: "Umph!" But then she gave him that head tilt and flutter again. "Hmmm… I am being reminded of a similar situation we faced several days ago. And I feel this compulsion to ask… What are the chances that one good lickin' just might be followed by another?"

Larry growled teasingly in response. "I would say that the chances are about 110%."

Her eyes arched once more. "Well, I wouldn't be surprised if in the aftermath of all of this happening this morning, you did not find yourself… totally… and completely… blown…… away."

He looked at her through narrowed eyes: "Across my knees, young lady."

She gave him a smart salute: "Yes, sir!" She fluttered her lashes as she began to lower herself across his knees, then whispered to him: "Let the licks begin".

~~~

Bart and Deb lay intertwined and naked on his bed, her bottom red and glowing in the dusky late morning light allowed in by the closed curtains. Their expressions were mutual combinations of surprise, emotional exhaustion and most of all, contentment and satisfaction.

She sighed deeply and murmured as Bart ran his hand down her hip and thigh. "I'm so happy that I brought that lotion in my purse. I guess I just anticipated needing it to soothe the pain I was expecting… I must add, the pain I indeed received."

She laughed for a moment. "I just never expected that asking you to apply it would result in… All I can say is… Yippee…Yay…Wow!".

Bart laughed and pulled her close and kissed her. "You can't say enough good things about unplanned joys. I know that I'm quite pleased right now."

She laughed and shook her head. "I never would have noticed."

He measured his words carefully for a moment. "I need to warn you… I'm thinking I might like to be able to do this with you for the rest of my life."

Tears formed in her eyes immediately. "I may agree to that."

They kissed long and hard and he shook his head. "We seem to be resolving all kinds of matters this morning."

She ran her hand over his shoulder: "it's been a morning full of sensations I haven't felt for a long time. And now I know what it feels like to make love without worrying about getting pregnant."

Bart laughed and nodded his agreement: "To say nothing of finding out how much it hurt to get whacked with the old high school paddle."

She cringed and squeezed her eyes shut for a moment: "Well, Bart, I was really not fully forthcoming this morning. You see, at least in the past, there was always what was called Senior Prank Day.

"So, it seems that when the day came around the year I graduated, Mr. Powell decided that myself and four of my classmates took things a little too far in regard to some spray paint. And that was how that one year it became known afterward as 'Seniors Got Spanked Day...".

THE END

The Suggestion

Trevor and Connie Mason sipped wine after yet another late weekday dinner of take-out food from a local pulled pork and brisket barbecue restaurant. The day had been long for both of them, but it had also been profitable for the two thirty-year-olds who were doing quite well in operating their own tiny firm. Just four years earlier they had both left other agencies performing in the busy housing market that was the Atlanta metropolitan area. In fact, they had met five years earlier at a local realtors' luncheon where home value appraisal was a program topic of the day.

It had seemed to be almost too good to be true: two people meeting at a punch bowl and striking up a conversation and having sparks fly. Twelve months later, they were married. And then the year after that, they decided to establish their own fledgling appraisal firm to serve the real estate agencies and banks in the business of lending money for mortgages.

They seemed to be a good fit right from the beginning. On their first formal date they joked that probably not many people they knew would find real estate and property appraisal to be a fascinating line of work. However, both of them did, and that seem to hasten the development of their relationship.

People liked to call upon them to do their appraisal work throughout the Atlanta area largely because of the reputation. They were known for being prompt, accurate, and very easy to work with. Even the more demanding real estate agents and bankers with reputations for being prickly sung their praises.

They even appeared to belong to each other. Trevor was just over six feet tall with an athletic, wide shouldered frame, along with his well trimmed black hair and minimal beard and mustache. But when they were together, every male I was upon Connie. It was not that she was statuesque by any stretch of the imagination at 5'3" in height.

But she was very pretty with straight blonde hair that just fell down over her shoulders. She had a peaches and cream complexion to go with her blue eyes. If the phrase that a woman had a "girl next door" appearance, it would have been Connie.

Trevor and Connie were both quite aware that her persona, the combination of her looks and sweet disposition that seemed to melt away any ruffled feathers, added much to their success. For that matter, when there would be times where they thought that Connie could take advantage of her attributes to their benefit, she would take that meeting or that event, and Trevor would put his energies in another direction, such as lining up more work for them to do.

They simply had a reputation as a sweetheart couple. Most of the time that was fairly accurate in the description of their relationship that was now approaching its sixth year of marriage. But they were certainly having their moments!

When they had first begun working as a team, Trevor was just beginning to pick up some hints that Connie was proving to be a little difficult in some areas. Although they had never stipulated it to be part of her job responsibilities, soon after they formed their own firm she had taken it upon herself to be the unofficial examiner of completed forms and financial transactions.

It was not that Trevor had any tendency to be error-prone, no more than Connie. But Connie simply seemed compelled to want to examine every bit of paper that flowed through their office to look for discrepancies and errors. When she found something, she would bring it to Trevor's attention with more than a touch of attitude in the way she presented it.

Most of the time, it turned out that everything was fine the way it was. Plus, Trevor gave her credit for the fact that she double checked her own work just as closely as his. The problem was, she was exhausting herself and spending valuable time in checking for errors that were basically nonexistent by the very nature of them.

It was in the fourth year of their now nearly six years of marriage that her tendency started to become an issue that was being taken home with them in the evening. Trevor had tried on several occasions to explain to her that she was going overboard in critiquing his work for very little benefit in return for the energy she was expanding in that way.

But most of all, his concern was for the relationship. He was finding himself experiencing moments when he simply had a reaction similar to when someone would scratch their fingernails across the chalkboard when she would begin to discuss work after hours. And it was beginning to affect them in the bedroom as well.

They had no plans or desire to have children. But even though that was their choice from the beginning of the relationship, they had certainly enjoyed a mutual and ravenous sexual appetite. But in the past several months, that had started to wane because of the tension being carried home from their job.

For Trevor, the frustration was building, because each time that he tried to carefully word the beginning of a talk with Connie about the issues, her reaction was usually pointed and unreceptive, so things only got worse as the months went by.

Now Trevor's relationship with Connie's family was solid. And Connie held his family in very high esteem as well. In fact, Trevor's older sister Yvonne was not only close to her kid brother, but she and Connie had become the closest of friends. Yvonne and her husband Brad lived just five miles away in a different Atlanta suburb, and Yvonne and Connie would meet for lunch at least once per week to engage in girl talk.

It finally happened on a warm June day when they were sitting at an outdoor café table lunching on salad and iced tea that Connie confided to Yvonne that there were stresses in her marriage to Trevor. Now what had always impressed Yvonne about Connie was the fact that her younger sister in law was always quite open and candid, and never seemed to beat around the bush when something needed to be discussed. That was one reason they had become confidantes for each other. The exception was any mention of Connie's nit picking on the job.

As they sat beneath the canopy, both of them tried to ignore the admiring gazes of a table full of men who had apparently just gotten there after a morning on the golf course. Apparently, they were seeing a lot to appreciate about Connie in her short yellow shift dress, and Yvonne in the blue. red and yellow flowered sundress, a wonderful contrast with the long brown wavy tresses that fell down upon her shoulder.

They giggled between themselves for a moment in feeling flattered by the attention they were getting, but then Connie cleared her throat and began to talk about more serious matters.

Yvonne set her fork down and listened with concern and an open mind as Connie began to relate her feelings about what was putting a strain in their marriage. Right away, Yvonne reached over and patted Connie on the shoulder when she saw that Connie was being remarkably open and honest about the manner in which she was bringing the problems upon the marriage, and how she had dismissed Trevor's attempts to talk to her in a reasonable manner.

Connie poured out her heart for a while, realizing as she talked that it was her own stubbornness and insecurity that was putting up a barrier between she and Trevor. And then Connie began to cry as she told Connie how much she deeply loved Trevor, and wanted to make things better.

As she poured out her heart to Yvonne, Connie could see a very understanding expression on her sister-in-law's face, one that almost indicated that Connie was not relating anything to Yvonne that she had not perhaps been through herself. And when Connie was done venting her anxieties and concerns, Yvonne reached across the table and took both of her hands in hers and grasp them firmly.

"I want you to know, I would always be willing to talk to either of you, or both of you about these things if I could be of help. Of course, the last thing that I would want to do would be to interject myself into your marriage. I would never want to go beyond where I was welcome. She laughed for a moment. "I know that sometimes when I get started with my infallible advice, I don't know when to stop."

Both of them were giggling as Connie considered her response. "Yvonne, I came to learn very quickly that Trevor treasures your opinion on almost anything. I would be very pleased if Trevor would agree for you to sit down with the two of us as an objective person and maybe help us avoid something we might regret later."

~~~

After dinner that evening, Trevor knew something was up when Connie seemed somewhat subdued, then asked him to join her on the living room sofa with their wine so that they could talk in more comfort. He agreed, and as they walked to the living room, his heart raced with fear at what she may have to say about the future of their relationship.

But once they sat down, Connie kicked off her shoes and drew her feet up on the sofa and curled up against Trevor. Then she began a long narrative about the lunch discussion she had had with his sister. Trevor could see right away that she seemed to be experiencing a great deal of relief as she went on.

He was somewhat surprised to hear her references to her acknowledgment of the problems she had brought on, and referred to her realization as being "long overdue". That was when she got to the heart of the matter: "Yvonne has offered to sit down with the two of us and help us to work through some of the things that are getting in our way.

"Brad would not be a part of it, and Yvonne said that he was not the type to want to offer advice in someone else's marriage. But tomorrow is Friday, and I looked at both of our calendars. She has tomorrow off from the beauty parlor, and it looks like both of us could be free around lunchtime.

"If it's okay with you, I would like to call her right now and take her up on her offer. I think it would be good if the three of us could sit down tomorrow over lunch, right here at home, and see if we can perhaps get rid of some of these issues that have been putting a barrier up. What do you say?"

Trevor blew out a deep breath of relief. "Connie, I can't tell you how happy I am to be having this conversation with you. I've been getting really concerned about us, and I think that since we both have so much confidence in Yvonne's advice, we should certainly go ahead and do that."

He could see tears forming in her eyes as she reached to the coffee table to pick up her phone. Then he listened as the two women exchanged words of cautious happiness that they were going to be getting together the next day to talk.

Right before the conversation ended, Trevor heard Connie respond to something that Yvonne had said, although she laughed before giving her answer: "Yvonne... I think I can live with that."

She listened again for a moment. "No, no... I think that what we need is your honest opinion, and whatever it is that you think you're going to say that might freak me out, I don't want you to worry about it. What we need is your honesty, not someone telling me what I want to hear, or being afraid to tell me things that I need to hear but don't want to." She laughed once again in response to something else that Yvonne had said, then they said goodbye.

She set her phone down on the table again and shook her head. "Your sister seems to think she might say something tomorrow that is going to send me running and screaming away from the house."

She turned toward Trevor and put her arms around his neck and planted a kiss on his lips. "The only screaming I intend to do is in response to things I would like for you to do to me in our bedroom right now." Her expression grew more serious for a moment. "Trevor, I know it's been a while... I don't like for us to be that way. Want to go to the bedroom and try to make up for some lost time?"

<center>~~~</center>

When they got out of bed in the morning, they disappeared into separate bathrooms, then converged in the kitchen where they made breakfast together. It was something that had not happened for quite some time, and was a fitting follow-up from the night before when all kinds of things took place that had not occurred for a while in their house.

Finishing her breakfast quickly, Connie patted Trevor on the shoulder and left the kitchen, then returned in a moment with her phone: "I'm looking at both of our schedules for today. I don't know if you realize it or not, but neither of us have anything scheduled for after 10:30 this morning.

"And Yvonne's coming for lunch...".

Trevor smiled and put his arm around her waist as she stood next to him. "So maybe we should just keep our calendars open and have a slightly longer weekend than normal?"

Connie nodded eagerly and with an expression of expectation as she awaited another comment. Finally, he smiled and nodded in agreement. "I think that's a good idea. We haven't done anything like that for a while, and maybe we can have a whole weekend of enjoying ourselves for a change."

Connie plopped down on his lap, then crossed her legs in the short blue shift dress, causing him to comically growl in appreciation as he moved his hand back and forth across her exposed right thigh. "Oh, I think we can think of things to do over the weekend, all right. And I can't remember the last time we have been to a movie, or we can go to a museum or just go to a mall and walk around like people who weren't driving themselves crazy with earning money."

She leaned to him in a kiss, then their arms were around each other tightly before she finally pulled away several inches and smiled at him. "Oh, my goodness. I could use a lot more of this normal couple time. I wish I didn't have to leave right now, but I have that rambling house up on Mason Memorial Ridge to evaluate."

They exchanged another kiss, then she reluctantly got up from his lap, reached for her purse from the kitchen counter and looked at him wistfully. "I know we can get through this, Trevor."

He had to fight the tears from overflowing his own eyes. "We will. We will do whatever it takes."

She bit down on her lip and felt as if she was beginning to tremble. "And I will do whatever is necessary. Trevor, I've come to realize that I have made all this much more difficult than it needed to be. And I'm feeling kind of overwhelmed with the sensation of unfinished business.

"I feel very responsible for a lot of things, and I know we are going to have to come up with some way to help me feel that we have dealt with at all and moved on. Because right now, sweetheart, I'm feeling a lot of weight on my shoulders that somehow needs to be lightened. Whatever it takes... Trevor... I mean that, whatever it takes."

Even though they were going to have a shortened day, between the time they left the home early that morning and until they arrived within minutes each other back at the house right at noon, they had seemed to have packed in a full day. And just as both of them were getting out of their cars after their almost synchronized arrival, Yvonne pulled into the circular driveway in front of their house, stately in appearance with its stone construction, but not really that large with more than enough space for the two of them.

They went inside and sat down at the dining room table, Connie and Trevor serving out plates full of salad and spaghetti and meatballs Trevor had picked up on the way home. They made small talk while they ate, and then when they were finished, the dirty dishes were quickly placed in the sink.

In spite of the time of day, Trevor poured them small glasses of wine. Then they sat down for a serious discussion

Trevor and Connie could both sense the reluctance in Yvonne's expression as she tried to begin. "I want both of you, especially you Connie, to understand that some thoughts that I have to offer to you today are not very easy for me to say.

"I hope you took seriously what I told you on the phone yesterday evening, Connie because I'm probably going to say some things that you're not expecting to hear."

Connie assumed that Yvonne was going to make reference to what she certainly had seen at times to be Connie's intransigence when it came to changing some of her more unproductive habits. "I meant it, Yvonne... I need to hear what you have to say... I mean to say, we both have to hear what you have to say."

Yvonne took a sip of her wine in a manner that Trevor and Connie both found funny, and then she waited until the laughter had stopped, cleared her throat and folded her hands in front of herself. "Connie, I appreciated so much when we had our talk over lunch, just how willing you were to finally deal realistically with some of the issues. You may note that I use the word finally.

"I don't know if you recall that there were times when I tried to relate some of my observations that concerned me, but you seemed to shut down those attempts."

Connie bit down on her lip, took a deep breath and nodded emphatically so that both of them would see her acknowledgment that what Yvonne was saying was correct. "Connie, I have to be very blunt... I have been in the presence of the two of you when I have seen you be unnecessarily critical of Trevor.

"I say that at risk of having it appear that I'm simply taking sides with my kid brother. But I would be just as quick to make critical remarks of him. Trevor knows I have made a lifetime of doing that." They all began to laugh before she continued.

"So Connie, I do want to offer you guys a suggestion as to what I would recommend you do. And I'm going to tell you this by way of telling you a little story about something that happened between Brad and I four years ago. As a matter of fact, it took place just after you two had observed your first anniversary, I believe on the same weekend.

"I'm certain that Trevor remembers when I nearly wrecked something... I should say some things of great importance. Brad and his partners had formed their new law firm about eighteen months earlier, and then one evening Brad told me that he needed to have a talk with me.

"He had become aware that I had been a little too free and loose with my comments to and among some of the other attorneys' spouses at a couple of social functions. There were simply a couple of them that I just plain despised.

"I think that perhaps it was because I felt a little self-conscious because I was the only one of the spouses that didn't have a college education. I guess I felt kind of inferior, and I found myself engaging in unnecessary arguments, and worst of all, gossip, about and to some of the others.

"Brad had talked to me about it, but I kind of resented that, feeling that he was just another, better educated person trying to put me in my place. I just wasn't listening. Then there came a very awful day.

"Of course, on the other hand it may have been the best day of my life, considering what the events of that day ended up salvaging. But it turns out that on that Thursday morning when Brad got to the law office, there was an emergency memo on everyone's desk that the senior partner had called a special mandatory attendance meeting for lunch in the conference room.

"Any appointments that would have interfered with anyone being in attendance had to be canceled. Everyone knew that there was some kind of a crisis. Of course, there was something that had been keeping the pot boiling in that law firm, but they didn't expect the meeting to be about that.

"The time comes for the meeting to start, and they're filling their plates with a catered cold cut lunch that had been hastily arranged, and the senior partner starts talking about...me! Brad told me that he felt about two inches tall as all eyes turned toward him as the boss tried as politely and inoffensively as possible to explain to everyone there that the issues among the spouses was becoming too distracting for the firm to operate properly.

"Brad said it took every bit of courage she had to stand up and interrupt the boss. He just straight up asked if the discussion and meeting was solely about the problems that his own wife had been causing. He said that a look of sadness came over that senior partners' face, and he simply nodded his head in response to Brad's question.

"Brad then said he took a deep breath and made the boldest statement he had ever made: he announced to all of them there that when the next week rolled around, if there were any more problems being created by his wife, he would leave the firm and wish everyone else well.

"He went on to tell them that he was very sorry, and he went on to apologize about my behavior. Then he told them that he was going to take, and I quote… 'Decisive action'…that was either going to result in a cessation of my bad behavior, or his quietly packing up his belongings and vacating his office to make way for someone else."

Trevor and Connie were both shaking their heads in disbelief, and Trevor reached to his sister and clasped her hand. "I had no idea all that had gotten so serious. Brad was not about to whine about it to me I suppose."

Yvonne laughed and her face turned a deep shade of pink. "Oh, and don't get me wrong, he didn't whine about it to me either. But when he got home that evening, he had to wait for a couple of hours before my evening at the parlor was done. So, he had a lot of time to consider exactly how he was going to deal with me.

"I should clarify that. He had already decided that day how he was going to deal with me, but I think that some of the logistics in his planning were still unsettled.

"So when I walked in the house that evening, and saw him standing there with his hands on his hips and that very scary glare in his expression, I kind of felt my knees go weak. He walks up to me and puts his hands on my shoulders, but then he kissed me before he said anything.

"Then he told me everything about what had happened at that meeting. And I started crying, because I felt so horrible. I couldn't fathom the embarrassment that Brad had to feel at that meeting.

"So when he told me to go on to the bedroom and go ahead and get dressed for bed, I knew he wasn't talking about romance. And at the same time, I shifted into high denial gear and I was trying to erase from all probability what was really going to happen to me.

"I was just stunned at that greeting, and I began to walk slowly toward the bedroom, then he called out to me to stop and turn around. I must say, when he did that, I felt my blood turn cold. It's not that I thought Brad would hurt me... Well I need to clarify that... I was just very confused and disappointed in myself.

"Then he told me to have the hairbrush ready, and that he would be there in a couple of minutes."

Yvonne could not help but enjoy the dropped jaws she was looking at that moment. "Yes, that's exactly what was going to take place. So, I went into the bedroom, took off all my clothes and then just let a little nightshirt slide down over me. I made a very fast trip to the bathroom, and then when he arrived in the bedroom, I was sitting there on the edge of the bed holding the hairbrush. He had never before paddled me.

"He stepped forward and I just kinda' slumped my shoulders and handed the brush to him. He walks over to the dresser and pulls out the chair I always sat on when I was doing makeup or brushing my hair, and he sits down.

"I didn't even wait for him to say anything more to me. I just shook my head at my own thoughtless behavior and walked over and draped myself right across his knees. And he didn't waste any time.

"All of a sudden, that nightshirt was not where it had been a few seconds earlier, and that hairbrush landed on my bare bottom with a sound like a gunshot. And every several seconds, he landed that hairbrush on my butt with enough heat and sting to get a good campfire started.

"Brad is a gentle and kind man. But I have to tell you, that paddling lasted a really long time. But the thing was, I felt so badly about what I had done, I never one single time yelled out to him to stop. Not once did I ask him to stop paddling me, or even to not whack me so hard.

"As I'm laying there across his knees getting my butt just set on fire, I knew that there was nothing I could go through that would be any more fitting than what he was doing to me at that moment. And when it was over, I was bawling like a baby, but I had laid there and accepted and absorbed exactly what I had coming.

"And I won't go into what happened later that evening as we… I guess you would say, reconciled…". All of them began to laugh. "But needless to say, Brad is still with that law firm. And I have not said another word of gossip either within that group or anywhere else for that matter." Once again Connie and Trevor were laughing at the expression on her face.

"So, Connie, I have been thinking for some time as I have been observing some things you have done that have made things unnecessarily difficult for Trevor. You see, Connie I think that you would greatly benefit from Trevor giving you a very long and hard paddling as well."

Trevor and Connie slowly turned to look at each other, their eyes open wide and both of their faces flushing as Yvonne continued. "I told you may want to run away screaming from what I have to recommend to you. But what I recommend to the two of you, is that you go out this evening and have a nice dinner.

"Then following your dinner, you should go into a store… together… and look for the widest and most painful looking hairbrush you can find. And then, Trevor when you get home, you address Connie's problem in the same manner in which Brad addressed mine.

"And we would all hope for the same type of outcome." Her face turned pink. "And I mean that in every possible way." Her comment was followed by a round of embarrassed laughing. She folded her hands together in front of her. "So, there you have my recommendation."

She looked at her brother and her sister-in-law with a look of determination. "And now, I'm going to leave the two of you to the rest of your day… and night.

"And whether you follow through on what I have suggested or not, I really hope that the two of you come to some kind of resolution about this problem you're having. And Connie, your friendship means so much to me… I hope that you don't feel offended by what I just said."

Yvonne got up from the table, and then immediately Connie rushed to her and put her arms around her and gave her a tight hug. And then to the surprise of all three of them, she leaned her head back and nodded resolutely and turned toward Trevor. "Were going to do that!" She took a deep breath and exhaled slowly. "And were going to do that tonight."

Then she turned to Trevor and held on to him tightly and began to cry softly. "You can do this, can't you Trev?"

He reached down and patted her on the bottom. "I promise I will give it everything I have." She pulled her head back and looked at him and winced, and in spite of the subject of the moment, she laughed softly.

CHAPTER 2

They sat in an ice cream parlor late that afternoon, spooning in dishes of plain and inoffensive vanilla. As she struggled to eat very much, Trevor stroked her arm. "I don't have much of an appetite either. Perhaps, after… I guess that what I'm saying is, I can fix us something at home."

Even under the circumstances, Connie was able to force a smile. "I think that your sister may be made of something different from me. I think she imagines that right now we are at a nice restaurant having a splendid meal, you in a sport coat and me in a nice dress. I can't imagine eating a lot right now.

"So here we are having some ice cream to help keep my stomach together, sitting here in jeans while I can't get my mind off our next stop along the way." She looked up at him and raised her eyebrows, then looked around to see that no one was near.

When she finally spoke, it was in a near whisper. "I can't explain why I would rather just be naked when I get my paddling."

Trevor continued to stroke her arm. "Actually, it will probably be more comfortable. For my part, it will probably make doing the job easier." She looked up at him and raised her brows. "And in any case, I've never been anything but anxious to see you naked."

Deciding she could eat no more, she moved the cardboard cup and plastic spoon aside. "So I guess that the logical place for us to stop is that hair and nail store a few blocks from our house? When I bought a round hairbrush, I never thought of needing a flat one."

Her expression grew somber. "But you know, if I had been paying attention to my own behavior, I may have long ago considered the need to have one around." She took one last sip of her diet soda and gave him a teasing kick to the ankle beneath the table. "And I'm thinking that we probably had better always have one ready, just in case of a Connie emergency of bad behavior."

They picked up everything from the table and walked it over to the trashcan, and Connie felt another wave of nerves as they got in the car to go on to the last stop before they would go home and she would receive what was undoubtedly going to be a paddling she would never forget.

It took them only twenty minutes to get to the rather large store that sold everything that a woman would want to take care of her nails and hair. When Trevor opened the door of the store for her to go in first, she felt a nervous shiver go up and down her spine, and felt as if her blood was running cool.

It was almost as if the sign on a side wall was calling out to them... "Brushes and combs". Connie felt as if her feet were made of lead as they walk slowly over toward a wall display of hairbrushes so generous that she felt as if some kind of karma was coming into play for how she had acted around and treated her husband over the past three or so years.

The section of hairbrushes made with wooden backs was almost shouting to her conscience, daring her to bypass the section of wooded hairbrushes she really deserved to select from in favor of a lighter, plastic flat brush. Trevor thought that he could hear her moan as she then sighed deeply and stepped over in front of the section of the models made from solid oak, with a sufficient width to justify calling what she was about to experience a true paddling.

She reached for one that was appearing to be the widest and longest, not encased in a plastic package, but simply on a peg, hanging by a string with a price tag that had been taped to the handle. She took it and held it, then turned it back and forth a few times and saw that Trevor was taking more interest in the brush than she wished that he would.

She slowly handed it to him, and he turned it back and forth a few times as well. She looked around then whispered to him. "Don't you dare slap that thing against your open hand, or I might just melt into a crying puddle right here in the store."

He shook his head and reached for his wallet as he began to walk toward the checkout counter. "You will be hearing the sound of the brush on bare flesh soon enough."

As a stood in line at the counter, she gave him a mild elbow to the ribs. "If you say or do something that makes me faint here in the store, you're going to have to carry me to the car."

But Connie did not faint. She stood next to Trevor as he paid for the brush, looking around and struggling to try to appear disinterested in the transaction. As they left, she felt that she had managed to act as casual as possible as she was standing next to a man purchasing a large wood hairbrush that he was going to be paddling her bare bottom with, all likelihood in thirty minutes or less.

They did not even attempt to have a conversation for the remaining ten minutes of their outing. Still not saying anything, but at least holding hands on their way from the garage inside to the house, once inside Trevor place the hairbrush on the dinette table in the kitchen and pulled her into his arms and gave her a long and deep kiss.

He looked down and brushed some hair from in front of her eyes. "I think that my sister was right about her suggestion. And I think that you are right to insist that it's what we need to do."

He kissed her once again. "Do you want to go ahead and get this done?"

She looked up at him and nodded, her eyes beginning to fill with tears. "How about you go to the living room and close the curtains, so we can do this on the sofa. And I'm going to go into the bedroom and take off everything, and then I'll meet you there." Trevor just nodded in agreement.

He watched her walk away slowly, then he picked up the hairbrush and made his way into the living room. He went around closing the blinds and curtains, then slid off his shoes just as his beautiful wife walked naked into the living room, everything else on her mind seeming to diminish any embarrassment she may feel. But after all, she was only being seen by Trevor, and she felt a sense of comfort in being that way in front of him.

They didn't say anything at first, simply communicating with each other with their eyes, and then he went to the sofa and sat down on the middle cushion. She stepped over to the coffee table in front of the sofa and pulled a couple of tissues from a box , gripped them tightly in her right hand and then stepped over to the sofa. She then lowered herself onto it and placed herself across her husband's knees for the first time, and honestly asking herself it would actually be the last.

She settled into place, then only a few seconds passed before she felt the hairbrush being slightly shuffled back and forth across her bare bottom. Then she heard him speak in a voice so soft she almost began to cry as he stroked her back: "It's going to start now."

She squeezed her eyes shut and clenched her teeth, and then the hairbrush landed across the left cheek of her bottom with an unnerving... WHAM...the affect of which was to provide a sting so hot that it took her breath away. She could not have cried out had she wanted to. But she really did not want to, even as they hairbrush returned with equal force, but this time to the soft, pink right globe.

All at once she was stunned by the pain produced each time the hairbrush impacted her naked backside, and at the same time appreciative of the barely perceptible, small amount of self recrimination that seemed to leave with each painful swat of the brush. As the hairbrush continued to arrive with fire and heat every several seconds, she found herself amazed that she had not cried out in any manner, considering the almost unbearable sensations raining down upon her.

It had not taken very many impacts of the hairbrush for tears to begin trickling down her cheeks. But just as she found herself surprisingly silent as each painful whack of the hairbrush arrived in a steady rhythm, several seconds apart, she realized that she was also crying in silence.

By the time the frightening... CRACK...had accompanied the scorching impact of the brush for the twentieth time, she knew that Trevor had to be feeling her body shake in tandem with her muffled sobs. But still it went on...and on.

It was when the unforgiving, unyielding oak rectangle had slammed down upon her now nearly crimson flesh for the thirty-fifth time, she finally cried out and began to sob loudly and frantically. And yet, she reached out in front and gripped the edge of the cushion and held on as tightly as she could. And for the next ten and final arrivals of the hard wood on her soft bottom, her verbal responses varied between squeals and yelps, but never once did she reach back and try to avoid or interfere with the arrival of the brush.

She suddenly realized that while his left hand was once again gently stroking her back, the right hand was no longer holding the brush, let alone bringing it down upon her bottom. Instead, it was gently and slowly cruising up and down the backs of her thighs, and she realized that Trevor had begun the process of helping her settle down and recover.

He thought that she would wish to remain in place for a moment, but instead he realized she was beginning to try to get herself back up into a kneeling position, so he helped her up and they were immediately embracing tightly. For three minutes, she was in his tight embrace as she laid her head on his shoulder and cried. Finally, he whispered to her that he would be right back, and she simply nodded her head in understanding.

When he got up from the sofa and began to walk back to their bedroom, he found that his own legs were rubbery, and his mind was racing a process if that had actually just taken place. When she saw him walking back into the living room, she stood up and forced a smile as he helped her into the light weight, silky white bathrobe that would cause her no additional discomfort, but also cover her and keep her warm.

Even as he tied the rope closed in front of her, she was still leaning her head on his chest and crying, and he kissed her on the cheek and ran his fingers through her hair: "Would you like to go and lay down for a while?"

She raised her head, her face blotches of red and white and her eyes rimmed a dark pink. "Will you lay down with me?" He simply put his arm around her waist and walked her into the bedroom.

He turned back the covers, then helped steady her as she laid down on her stomach, and then he took a place next to her. She was still sniffling, and reaching back and rubbing her bottom with both hands. He could never have put into words the relief he felt with an expression of contentment, rather than one of anger and rejection.

He was surprised to see a hint of a smile on her lips, but then understood when she spoke. "I have a jar of cold cream in my top drawer of my nightstand." Suddenly they were smiling at each other, something neither one of them would have expected ten minutes earlier. He got up and walked to her nightstand, and while he was up he rapidly undressed and put on his own pajamas.

He returned to his place next to her with the jar of the soothing cream, opened it and then shuffled her almost weightless robe up on her back. Then he opened the jar and scooped some of the cream on his fingertips and began to carefully and gently apply it to her bottom. As he did so, he had to struggle to not begin crying as his fingertips carefully smoothed the cream over the deeply red, substantial portion of her bottom that had been so thoroughly worked over by the brush.

He felt himself begin to tremble from this cascade of second thoughts that were now unsettling him. The extent of the heat radiating from her paddled flesh unnerved him, making him wonder if he had crossed the line into cruelty. But when she closed her eyes and began to murmur with contentment as he continued to apply the soothing cold cream, he found himself settling down and his sudden doubts were diminishing with each passing second.

The minutes that followed seemed surreal to Trevor. He applied more cold cream, and allowed his hand to roam all across the back of her body. But all the time, Connie hardly said a word. She simply lay there with her face turned toward him, resting the side of her head on her crossed arms.

There would be the occasional, residual sniffle, and Trevor would pick up a tissue and dab it to catch an escaping tear here and there. But it was the look on her face that he found almost mesmerizing. It was more of a gaze, an almost dreamlike state as she tried to comprehend what had brought them to that point.

There would be moments when he would be caressing her hip, or the backs of her thighs when a bit of a sigh would escape her, and the beginnings of a smile would tease both of them. Then there would be those moments when she would suddenly be sucking in her breath, or squeeze her eyes shut and bite down on her lower lip as unexpected but sharp twinge of a burning sting would ripple across her bottom.

That was when her eyes would begin to fill with tears once again, and it was one of those moments that caused Trevor to draw her to him and embrace her tightly. And then she extended her arms and wrapped them around him, and she whispered to him and asked if he would rub her bottom for her.

Trevor did nothing to make light of what had happened, nor to make any premature attempts at giving her any less time than she needed. There had probably never been a time in their marriage when he had simply held her for so long, with so much of the time enveloped in a silence so stark that all he could hear was her breathing, breathing that was finally becoming once more soft and un-labored.

It was probably an hour after the last time the hairbrush had brought its burning sting upon her when they finally began to have a bit of a talk. And once it began, it went on for a long time.

She talked about the things she had done and the way she had acted, and how she had realized the night before after talking to Yvonne, that for some reason she had finally grasped the seriousness of it all. She finally laughed at one point when she remarked that a part of her could have been spared a major trauma had she allowed both Trevor and Yvonne's words to register in her mind even just a few months earlier.

Then she made another comment that left her feeling confused by her own words. "And at the same time… I feel now that… I feel that maybe it's just as well that what just happened came to pass."

She could see the look of surprise and confusion on Trevor's face before she continued: "I don't want to ever go through anything quite that… I'm not sure what I'm saying, Trevor.

"You know, my dear husband… I just need to trust you more. If I had trusted you the way I should have, then this issue of my nitpicking your work would never have become an issue.

"And if that had not become an issue, I wouldn't be feeling right now like my butt is in flames. At the same time, I really don't resent one little bit what just took place."

She laughed softly and began to run her hand over his cheek. "You see, I think there are worse things than to come to realize that you have a husband who does have a line that can't be crossed. But in your case, Trevor, I took advantage of you, because you are too kind and considerate to draw that line and put the hammer down… I should say hairbrush… I need to experience when I go past it.

"So in a strange kind of way, I feel comforted by what just happened. I hope you understand what I mean by this… I found out that if push comes to shove, you are willing to put an end to nonsense. And at the same time, you seem to have possession of an uncanny ability to know when you have taken me right up to the line.

"I'm saying in a clumsy way that that's just another way that you proved to me just how much I can trust you. I hope I never earn another paddling like the one I just got, but I'm saying something I can't believe coming out of my own mouth… I don't want you to ever lose track of where we keep that hairbrush."

Then she stopped talking and snuggled in more tightly against him. He continued to stroke her for a while, until he felt that she was ready to move on: "So what sounds good for you to eat? I would imagine that by now you may be starting to feel like having me fix you something?"

She leaned up and looked at him and managed to grin. "Scrambled eggs and toast. Lots of butter on that toast."

He planted a kiss on her lips and then tousled her hair. "You can stay here and rest if you want. I'll come get you when it's finished." He went to get up, but she reached out to him, put her arm around his neck and drew him to her and she kissed him on the lips. Then he heard her soft voice: "Thanks for what you just did for me... I mean all of it."

~~~

He decided to give her some space, even a chance to cry a little more in private, so he took his time. Thirty minutes since he had left the bedroom, he reappeared with a tray full of scrambled eggs, toast and glasses of juice. He placed the tray on the floor, then scurried about gathering up pillows so that Connie could rest her upper torso over them while eating breakfast without having to sit.

She smiled at the extent to which he was trying to help her deal with the after effects of the rather dramatic paddling he had applied to her backside. And once he had her settled in with her meal, he sat down next to her with his own plate.

She looked over at him and managed to smile. "You can really cook... you can really paddle a woman's ass. You're a man of many talents."

He looked over at her, and she could see the distress in his expression as he spoke slowly. "Given the choice of the two, I would rather cook for you."

She reached over and placed her hand on his. "You're not starting to think that I didn't deserve that, are you?"

He looked at her with the stone sober expression for a moment, then allowed himself a wide grin and a wicked arch of his brows. "Not for a minute." Then he tousled her hair once again, and they went back to finishing their meals.

When they were done eating, he took their dishes, placed them back on the tray and returned them to the kitchen. When he came back to the bedroom, Connie had tossed some of the extra pillows on the floor, and was laying on her stomach in her normal position.

To his great relief, she saw him approach and patted the bed next to her.

Once he was resting next to her again, she displayed another hint of a smile and held up the jar of cold cream and handed it to him. He allowed himself a laugh and quickly brushed the robe up onto her back once again and began to apply the soothing substance.

He was still bothered somewhat in understanding that, even when morning came, her bottom cheeks were going to still be quite red, and sitting was going to be painful for her. He was still somewhat astonished at the warmth that still rose from the generous area that the hairbrush had impacted so many times with such velocity.

He did not know if he had ever heard a more welcome sound than her murmurs of contentment as he slowly and methodically went about smoothing the cold clean over her, obviously in no hurry to have that task finished. He thought that his heart was going to burst with affection and a certain amount of relief when she whispered with a wink of her eye: "That feels so good. You can do that all night."

He laughed and caught himself just before he was about to give her a teasing slap to the bottom, something he often did in moments of either relaxation or when they were enjoying a build up to some romantic mischief. Instead, he leaned over and kissed her while his hand continued the gentle application of the cold cream.

"Your eyelids are looking heavy."

She looked back at him and groaned dramatically. "I can't tell you how exhausting it is to have somebody tan your hide so expertly and effectively. I may end up drifting off into an early bedtime."

He continued his relaxing stroking of everything on the back of her. "It would probably be good for you. Don't try to fight it." She murmured something he could not understand, and then she was out for the night.

~~~

"How did you know I would still be hungry for scrambled eggs and toast this morning?" She had just woke, still on her stomach in the wisp of a robe, watching as he sat another tray of food on the top of his dresser, this time a carafe of coffee and two cups included.

He looked over at her and smiled. "I had to guess." She turned over and began to sit up against the headboard, then winced and sucked in her breath. This time, she laughed at herself as he unfolded a bed tray he had brought from the closet and placed it over her lap.

Then he did the same for himself and sat snuggled up against her as they enjoyed breakfast. He waited until they were done eating and sipping at their coffee. "So how are you this morning?"

She nearly spit out the sip of coffee she had just taken. "Are you talking about me overall, or the part of me that is still hot and sore?"

"Well…".

She took another sip and nodded her head. "I'm going to be very upfront about this with you, honey. I'm in exactly the shape I deserve to be, all things considered, after exactly what I needed last night. And I just hope that I have learned my lesson."

He put his arm around her shoulder, and she leaned her head next to his. "I can't remember the last time we took a shower together."

They turned slowly toward each other and began to laugh. Trevor slipped out of bed, folded up the lap tables and tidied everything up while she went into the bathroom. By the time he returned from the kitchen, she had the water adjusted and was awaiting him to join her in the large shower stall.

He was naked and beside her in an instant, and once under the pulsating streams, they were lathering each other with shower gel.

But it did not take long before they were embracing and enjoying a deep kiss.

She gazed up at him, chewing on her lips. "I have to ask you this for some reason…I thought maybe it would have turned you on to paddle me…I guess I just assumed it was something a guy would get a rush out of doing. But it wasn't?"

He blushed and laughed softly. "I guess it sounds sexy to give a spanking for fun. But that last night…it was no fun for me at all. I really let you have it."

She laughed and shook her head as she reached back to rub her still dark pink and warm bottom. "Gee, that's a surprise to me." Then she leaned up on her tiptoes and kissed him as they both laughed.

"You know, big fellow, I wouldn't be offended if spanking me turned you on. I have to tell you, as much as you were setting my butt on fire, I could not ignore that the warmth of it all seemed to be traveling all over the place down there."

Now they were both laughing again as Trevor opened his eyes wide: "You know, if you start to like that, I may start thinking of spanking you in a whole different light."

She pressed up against him and giggled. "Seems to already be taking effect."

She stepped behind him and reached her hands to his lower abdomen, slowly lowered them and allowed her fingertips to get to work.

~~~

Several minutes later they were next to each other on the bed once again, their skin still damp as Trevor slowly caressed Connie's bottom. "So I was picking up a hint in the shower that you are having your own moments of feeling kind of turned on while your backside was getting walloped?"

Her face turned dark pink and she nodded almost imperceptibly. Trevor wiggled his eyebrows at her, and coaxed her onto her back and begin to give her breasts a slow but thorough work over with his lips and tongue, all the while his left hand reaching down and stroking her abdomen, but also slowly moving his hand lower as he continued.

Soon his lips and tongue began to trace the downward journey of his hand as Connie began to giggle and moaned in excitement and anticipation. It was not long before her own loud moans and writhing in her own release filled the room.

~~~

Twenty minutes later they were standing next to each other in front of the stove preparing French toast. When they had shuffled the golden brown slices onto a plate, turned off the burner and moved the skillet was side, Trevor placed their breakfast on the small dining table in the kitchen.

Before they could sit down, they leaned forward and kissed once again, and Connie giggled as she afterward reached inside Trevor's mouth, took hold of his tongue wiggled it back and forth several times. "I wonder if your sister ended up getting anything nearly as pleasant after her paddling as I just did."

Trevor winked. "And as you are possibly going to receive again after the nice fun little spanking I plan to give you after breakfast."

Connie's eyes opened wide. "You know something, my special Trevor, I may just have to keep showing you some attitude from time to time if this is the penalty I'm going to pay."

THE END

www.ingramcontent.com/pod-product-compliance
Lightning Source LLC
Chambersburg PA
CBHW031249101125
35195CB00071B/1216